It is the Fall

The Lost Journal from Colorado

by James

An American College Novel ... plus Vietnam and
25 years floating through Steamboat Springs with
alcohol and drugs from 1965-1990
including poetry and prose.

Edited by J. Richard Johnson

Dedication

This book is dedicated to Raven

And

To friends whose journey in this life ended way too soon.

Rumor roars with a tremor
Of irrevocable momentum:
The shockwave seldom lethal,
The fallout generally fatal

By James, 1978.

Forward

I can't believe it's been nearly one quarter of a century since James left Steamboat Springs and he has finally allowed me to edit and publish some of his journal. In all this time he always wanted to publish a book of his poetry, but I knew that, while I enjoyed some of the poems, a book of poems just wouldn't sell.

The truth is that James is the type of person best described as a romantic dreamer. He just doesn't want to settle down in the real world and function as a normal person. He won't let himself grow up. If it weren't for me, in fact, he never would have gotten or held on to any of the jobs he ever had. I've always tried to be the practical thinker with at least some sort of financial planning involved in my decisions.

It's as though James and I are one in the same. I mean he did bring me a good amount of joy and laughter with his dreams and attempts to live in the woods like some sort of Indian. But at least he had me to keep him balanced enough so he wouldn't be locked up. I'm pretty sure I saved his life, perhaps gave him a new one, by convincing him to forget living in the past, start facing reality, sell his property and just get on with his life.

But now, after reading all this, I'm not so sure he wasn't correct. I'm thinking of letting him take over my being again. Those floating experiences were some of the best times I ever had. And if you don't believe us, don't think you're going to get answers by asking any questions. Perhaps you just need to meditate a little longer and look a little harder within.

Even though James believes everything in his journal really happened, he still wanted me to list this book as fiction so he would never have to answer any questions. Of course, I would have listed it as fiction anyway because who can truly believe that one could remember facts and dialogue well enough under the influence of drugs and alcohol to actually keep a journal? Besides, his mental state is not what I would deem as normal or balanced.

J. Richard Johnson,
Editor

When a poet dies, so too the flowers

It is the fall.
I see and smell the autumn leaves
as they gently twirl and circle,
looking for a spot
on grassy ground.

Cherish red and honored gold;
haunted green and mellow-yellowed
crispy patterns, aspen, spruce and pine.
Drying garlic, sage and beef;
melting wax on potbelly stove
heated after morning's grass –
"Toke it to me, man.
"I'll take a poke of mind's soap
 before a cup of tea anytime!" I laughed.
Gathering mint for winter's tea
and leaving thoughts to pass

A breeze picks up and they rustle along,
those drying memories of youthful spring.
Gone now is the strength and fullness
of rich-spent summers:
caked and crinkled, covered with dust.

Yet when all are gone or hidden
beneath new fallen snow,
and when white again pretends
illusion of freshness and season of merriment,
who can forget the joyous memory
that leaves have left?
And their dry-sound rustle in passing winds,
or tranquil brushes with one another.

James 3

Twirling, spinning twisted masses,
making passes,
leaves entwine my mind;
Tiny bits of thoughts and laughter
drying on mind's line.

Thus passed the season that year – the year of the fall. Now
the winds howl and whistle, branches shuddering in barren shame.
The leaves were truth, not passing fancy; their beauty could be seen
and touched and smelled. (The wind alone, it has no sound.)

So true of man as a leaf
and of a family, type or breed.
This forest is a nation,
and many are a world;
some pass on and others sprout:
They ask but cannot hear...
for now it is the winter.
So true a man he knew a leaf,
and still a bud, a root.
Now he is your soil.

Looking back, I wonder how long all things seemed past and
future, never knowing present. But isn't that the way with all?
Wondering what it is that seems to make us be this way or that.
Wondering where we're going, whose choice that is and whose voice
it is that seems to speak us to that point when all things become as one.

Sometimes I think
I never sat beside a brook
and listened
to its gentle murmur
watched
the rushing ripples

smoothing glass and stone
to sand.
Nor gazed upon the lilies,
smelled
the berries
touched
the bark,
thought
of freshness,
stillness
and filtered rays of
warming sun.
Often I wonder
of the many joys
of childhood
that seemed to pass
so fast.

I'm perfectly normal sane just like you. There's no point in
deliberating that fact. That has been considered, contemplated,
almost to the point of absurdity. Of course that may be just the
problem, but I think not. Not any more anyway. It's just the
thoughts, the one and two line blurbs, the burps of information, the
questions that keep popping up from somewhere.

And the mind-blowing answers. If, I mean, I'm even correct
in assuming that's what they really are. "They? Tiny bits of truth?"
I ask. But then why must I still believe that there is an answer,
waiting, or even moving, but there somewhere, begging to be found.

Not alone along the solemn isles I trod,
out beneath the fading palms and drying grass.
Hardly alone with quiet sun and smell of salt and sea.

But then what is it? What is becoming of me – and of all men?

I suppose you could say it's the old, "What can you say about six semesters at a private, four-year liberal arts college in a small Midwestern city?" gambit.

Shall I talk about fraternity life, the college bar, girls I dated, parties, booze, midnight capers, near busts and sometime trusts; a part in a play and the cast party; spring vacations at Daytona, Ft. Lauderdale, Miami and Bimini; illegal rushing and hell week and lineups; a gang bang, a touch on mono; the formal dance, and the barn party complete with strippers and stag films (the lights went on and we caught the farmer masturbating); a lay by the railroad tracks as a freight train went by; late night cramming and bullshit circles and more cramming and red devils and yellow jackets; the first sit-downs and the first arrests (the barber claimed he didn't have scissors to cut "their" type of hair); vandalism and peeping toms and panty raids and homecoming and how many coffees, teas and hot chocolates?

And, of course, there were cigarettes and beer nuts, Slim Jims and peanut shells; fake ids and a job on the school newspaper; folksongs and songfests and sunbaths and snowballs; drive-ins and eight ball and bowling; automats and Laundromats; sorority sisters; rumors and legends; weekends home and away, walkouts and lockouts; traffic accidents; doctors' notes; tea with a teacher, pledge songs and sons and chapter meetings; basketball (our team was drunk), football games, baseball, track, swimming and handball; ROTC, long lectures, beavers and blouses, breasts and cheeks; one-eyes, round-eyes, universal flying frog kicks and gross-outs, water balloons and paint; the Holiday Inn after a formal; a midnight swim, ties and blazers and sweaters lost, borrowed and burned; early morning carousing, streaking and freaking; the divorced nymph and stewardesses; hours in art classes with smell of paint and clay; home in the summer and back in the fall; issues without answers, TV and the death of JFK; convocations, entertainers, B's and D's; out-of-sight legs and calves and boxes from home and away and from New York and from L.A.

It was, in all, a pretty horrendous, happy, wasteful, enlightenly mellow, monetarily rewarding and disgustingly boring, mixed, happy-sad, intro-retrospective, novicely nice, six long and short semesters: halfway enjoyable, glad it's over, everything lost and gained, with too much to learn and not enough time – I never returned.

In Youth

As far back as I can remember, my first desire in life, after, of course, to be loved, was to be one with Nature. Sometimes, though, Nature didn't love me, or tried to frighten me, and I could never figure out why. Even to this day, I still wonder why Nature is so impersonal, so non-loving and indiscriminate in her relations with people. Nature can be so unthankful and ungrateful, in fact, that I often wonder why people love her so. Perhaps they love to forgive. Or maybe people love Nature just out of respect. One is rather obligated to respect anything that has power over him. Especially a power that will one day claim us all.

When I was young in a suburb of a city, there was a field across the street from my house. The field was four blocks deep and six blocks long, and in the summer it was a living, breathing jungle of smells and sounds. Often I pitted myself in battle against moths and grasshoppers, all colors of butterflies, and green "garter" snakes, baby rabbits and song birds and crickets.

Weeds grew high in the field; they were well over my head. When I was in my world – even just twenty feet along in a trampled path – I was suddenly alone with Nature. The sounds of life were so loud I could never hear the dinner bell. My senses were tuned to life.

Sometimes Chuckie would join me in the field and we would trample new paths, form trick mazes or dig three-foot holes and cover them with straw to trap unwary natives. Spears were whittled from dried weed stalks. We would break them off a foot from the roots and then pull up the stem with its clump of dirt and store the "bombers" in our ammo area. Frequently we would be attacked by big neighbor kids from the other side of the field. Then we'd run home, knowing they would tear down our fort.

Once I was hit between the eyes by a bomber that had a rock in its clump of dirt, and my face was bloodied. It didn't hurt, but I got a lot of attention when I got home because I might have lost an eye.

Chuckie and I made butterfly nets and caught all types of flying bugs; we kept them in peanut butter jars with nail holes in the lids. I kept my jars in the shade so the butterflies wouldn't "melt", then let them go in the evening after dinner. They looked much happier to be free again after their experience in captivity.

Often after supper, when it was too dark to play hide 'n' seek, Chuckie and I would catch lightning bugs and sneak them in jars up to our bedrooms. I remember one time my holes were too big and they escaped at night, flying all over the house.

The next summer, or maybe the one after, we didn't catch lightning bugs, but used to practice our swings at them with small baseball bats. Chuckie once got 47 of them in half an hour. I was wearing shorts and got eaten by mosquitoes.

Butterfly Nets and Boyhood

> Jungle fields of summer
> played magic with my head.
> White and yellow butterflies,
> a monarch as big as my net.
>
> Garter snakes gargantuan
> frightened the sissy girls;
> worms and beetles and caterpillars
> were friends to living hands.
>
> Lightning bugs in a Skippy jar
> were snuck up to many a bed
> but they always escaped by morning
> and I faced my mother with dread.
>
> Footprints on the dewy lawn
> left tracks while stalking the cat;
> the milkman knew my name then
> and swung my Hank Sauer bat.

When we were in the sixth grade, Chuckie and I tried to shoot blackbirds with our Daisy BB guns. Then once we shot a robin to death in old Mrs. Feenie's backyard and she called Chuckie's dad at work. When he got home that night he broke Chuckie's gun over his knee and said I shouldn't come over again for a week. I never told my parents about the bird, but I put my gun in the back of my closet and don't remember playing with it much again.

I remember when a neighbor moved in a few houses away on our street called Hamlin Avenue in Skokie, Illinois, before we moved to a better location. He called me the towheaded kid and I asked him about a million questions as his furniture was being moved in. My mother told me not to bother him because his name was Robert May and he wrote a book called Rudolph the Red Nosed Reindeer.

I miss watching westerns on TV on Saturday and Sunday mornings. And I miss my Davy Crockett blanket with "scenes of Davy in action on the mattress." I don't miss the knotty pine walls in my bedroom with every large knothole a face starring down at me. But I could always sleep in the hallway if they started talking.

The Factory

If what I hear and see in the movies is correct, high school is supposed to be one of the most memorable periods in one's life, full of magical moments and life-shaping awakenings. For starters I can say that if you are part Norwegian, measure 4'8" as a freshman, 5'8" as a senior, but grow four more inches in college, and if your high school has an enrollment of more than 3,500 students and is located in a wealthy suburb on the north shore of Chicago, chances are your influence has the same effect as a rock thrown into Lake Michigan and being noticed in Detroit.

On the plus side, my one good friend was shaving by the eighth grade and could easily purchase beer by our sophomore year. We spent our summer days drinking beer on the beach and watching each year as the teasing girls reached maturity. Excitement consisted of throwing a cup of cold water on their backs, causing them to sit up abruptly, then screaming while groping for their tops.

In the humid 90 degree heat of a Chicago summer, we could get pretty hammered on six beers apiece.

Taken all together, high school is a four-year blur of forced, non-elective classes crammed down my throat. Every class gives a minimum of one hour of reading every night and that doubles on weekends: six hours or more you are supposed to do on Friday night to have the weekend free, but which always gets put off until Sunday night after Ed Sullivan on television.

It doesn't help that my sister is three years older and gets straight A's for four years, thus leaving teachers to assume I am from the same mold and constantly calling me in to their offices to try to understand why I'm not applying myself.

The highlight of my freshman year is watching one of my sister's friends, Ann Margaret Olsen, sing "We're having a heat wave, a tropical heat wave" in the annual Lagniappe theatrical production.

I practice with the gymnastic team after school for three years on the side horse and high bar but am never good enough to get in a meet. But I do improve my biceps and beat out my gym class record for being able to hang from a high bar for something like 9 minutes straight. I weigh in at about barely 130 pounds, but can do sit-ups and pushups all day. There are starting football players who can't even do one chin on the high bar.

I figure the best part of maturing so late is that I don't have to worry about shaving around the blonde-haired plague of adolescent acne. The worst class is the four-week, once-a-year gym class where 60 guys have to stand freezing, naked and nude, starring at an Olympic-sized pool. Luckily my years of growing up swimming in Lake Michigan mean I can swim, float or tread water as long as anyone on the swim team.

Finally graduating from the factory is the happiest day of my life.

It is the Fall

A College Highlight

If I'd been smart, I would have gotten in on the pollution movement beginning with the first time I viewed the city. But that was back in 1962.

Besides the churning smoke of Caterpillar Tractor's "military-industrial complex," and the mighty smokestacks of Hiram Walker and Pabst Blue Ribbon and a number of other, smaller, growing concerns, the one thing that always struck me most about Peoria was the smell. Dubbed in college jargon, "the armpit of the world," Pe-u-oria always had an odor in which, depending on what suburb of the city one lived in and on the direction of the wind (when present), whole suburbs were known to change their moods in a matter of minutes. What started out as a beautiful, fresh spring day could suddenly turn into a putrid scorcher with no nasal relief in smell for hours. Unless, of course, one loved the aroma of fermenting barley and hops.

I remember my father firmly gripping the wheel and guiding the green caddie through the curves until we were riding parallel to the Peoria River. A hot, misty steam hung over the city across the river in the high-noon September sun.

"You know, I really envy you, James," he began again. "I never had a chance to go to college myself. In those days, you were lucky just to get through high school, and you had to be pretty sharp to get any kind of job at all."

"Yea, I know," I said, gazing out the window.

"So ok," he said, his face getting red again. "I just want you to realize what a break you're getting. A chance to get the kind of education I never had. And I'm hoping you'll do a good job."

I figured I already knew enough to teach a graduate course in "The theory of life as a sequence of breaks," by Dr. James

Knuckledown: "A subjective analysis of how to play the odds on your side, or life is merely a game. It's just that there aren't any rules." Some game.

We drove through town and up to the campus where a sign read, "Bradley University, founded by Lydia Moss Bradley, 1898." Then we were unloading my bags, walking up and down three flights of stairs in the new men's dorm and, finally, thirty minutes later, standing back by the car.

"Well, dad, I guess this is it," I said. "Thanks for everything."

"Ok James. Take care and get plenty of rest." He shook my hand firmly. I can't recall a time when we ever shook hands like that again.

I had that same old butterfly feeling in my stomach when I saw there were tears in his eyes. Then he got in the car, started it up and slowly pulled away.

I went upstairs, took off my sweater and T-shirt and looked in the mirror. One-hundred and thirty five pounds of skin and bone stared back at me. I washed up and lay down on the bed. College, I thought. Man. I finally made it. I'm here. Now my life begins. I lay there trying to comprehend the full meaning of these words and my present position in life. I fell asleep immediately.

The Paradox

> I never thought a circle
> but saw an arc without good taste,
> a slice of life I couldn't swallow,
> a side of man in mirror's
> non-reflecting face.
> Bad like good soon passes,
> and once again things meld,
> bringing together more of joy
> and sorrow than my mind
> can really handle.

But why, when to ask of one,
it seems so necessary
to invite the other?

The next day I attended "an assembly for all male freshmen."
We sat on the field house bleachers and listened quietly to a series of
lectures about this, the most important day in our lives.

"Men, as Dean of Men, I hope I never have to meet any of you
men personally in my office. (pause, ll laughs). All I want to tell
you today, men, is that you men don't know how lucky you are. You
were all hand-picked from thousands of applications. You men have
all proven by your high school records and by your SAT test scores
that you have the potential to graduate from this school."

"Right" I thought as his voice droned on. I had a C+ average
in high school and got in, in a snap. I knew a few guys with less
than a C average who were also accepted.

"But men, I want you to realize one hard, cold fact. Look
to the left of you. Now look to the right. One out of three of you
will not graduate from this college. And one out of four will never
graduate from college at all." (murmurs).

"You know why, men? Because some of you will flunk out.
Think about that fact, men. You can make it. But one out of four of
you won't."

"Now have a good time, study hard…and don't let me see you
men again – ha ha."

I was contemplating the dean's sense of humor when I heard
someone calling my name. It was Ken, a high school classmate
whom I barely knew. I was one who never understood the meaning
of the phrase, "how to cultivate friendships."

"Hey, I didn't know you were going here, Ken."

"Oh, I wasn't, but I didn't get accepted anywhere else," he
said. "Where are you staying?"

"Wycoff."

"Hey, so am I. Second floor."

"I'm on the third," I said, gazing at a good looking guy with a mop of brown hair.

"Cool," he said. "Oh, James, this is Mike from Whitefish Bay, Wisconsin."

"How ya doing, Mike," I said, giving him as hard a handshake as I could muster. "You staying in Wycoff?"

"Yea. Ken and I are roommates. Come on, let's grab some coffee."

We followed the flood of potential flunk-outs across the quad toward the student center. Mike, who was almost the same height as I, but weighed about 40 pounds more, began a long dissertation about why Whitefish Bay was the greatest suburb in the world. Ken, who hailed from Winnetka, as compared to my lowly Northfield, winked at me as Mike rambled on.

Still, Mike did mention some good points. And his supersarcastic sense of humor kept us laughing so hard we could barely get a word in.

"So, you balled a lot of women, James," Mike said, looking around and eyeing every girl in the place.

"Oh, I can't say I've balled a LOT of chicks," I said.

"Yea, I'll bet. I just wondered if they preferred you with or without that Clearasil on."

Ken and Mike really broke up over that one and people at surrounding tables looked over. I held a smile and looked back at them, trying to give the impression I'd just told a great joke. Some joke. Just wait, I thought. Like just wait for what?

"Look at the chest on the girl at the cash register," Ken said, pointing with his head.

"You mean that one," Mike said, standing up and taking a few steps toward her with outstretched arms. She suddenly looked over self-consciously and some thirty people who must have been watching started laughing. Real funny. So mature. But I was laughing right along.

Mike then went into detail about the girl he's been dating for the past year and a half, what a great lay she is and how she almost scratched his back off when he used his brother's French tickler on her.

"My brother only had one tickler, so he used to wash it out when he got back from a date with his girl, then leave it on the closet shelf to dry. My mother didn't get pissed at all when she found it – ought! Of course she probably made my old man use it on her that night. Anyway my brother broke up with this girl about a week later. Couldn't satisfy her any more without it."

Brushing his hair back, Mike continuously enlightened us about his older brother who taught him to box, about the advantages of growing up in a 3.2 beer state (where he had learned to drink at 15 via fake ids), how he loved to get into a good fight and about Muskego Beach where he heard Buddy Holly play. His real specialty, however, was putting people down. And at that he was a pro.

"James, huh. Blonde hair. Blue eyes. You're going to be real popular with the kikes around here," he said. "Look at the business teachers. Eight out of ten are Jews. Big chance you'll even make it through freshman year – ought. You better change your New Testament name or your major real quick."

"Yea, that's real funny" I said. "Still I mean a college professor isn't going to be prejudiced, is he?"

"Probably not if you ace every test."

I studied his round face with traces of a full beard. He certainly looked a lot older than the stupid 18 we all were.

"I think I'll put some quarters in the juke box," I said.

There was practically nothing but soul music on the juke box. I also noticed there were only a few black guys in the whole school and they were all as tall as any college kids I'd ever seen. I later found out Bradley excelled at one major sport: basketball. And in the '60s, thanks in part to generous alumni, the school could hold its own against any but the top 20 schools in the whole country.

That night we went to The Inn, a college bar about two miles from the campus. Although he almost didn't serve me because I look about 16, I later realized that Frank, the owner, served just about anyone who went to the university, except, of course a week before elections or when he got a phone call that there was going to be a raid in a half hour or so.

Frank drove an old dodge to work, but the word was that he owned two Cadillacs and his wife had a few furs and the biggest diamond you've ever seen. One look at the packed bar and it wasn't hard to see he was probably pulling at least 80 thou a year.

Evidently the cops figured the college students had to drink somewhere, so they might as well take their cut too. "Zero payoff" as Mike said.

I spent a lot of nights, as well as a lot of money at Frank's that first year at school. It was there that I learned my capacity for seven-sevens, screwdrivers, sloe gin fizzes, beer and even martinis when there was cause to display celebration – like passing or flunking an exam or finishing off a term paper.

I also picked up a lot of important information: a full moon would entail a car driving down the road with a bare ass sticking out all four windows, including the driver. Points are added if two eyes and a smile are painted on with lipstick; even more points if four cigars are worn appropriately. Universal flying frog kicks, however, entail the driver holding the gas with his hands and the shotgun rider steering, because the lower half of all four bodies must be hanging naked out the windows with the legs flaying in the air.

And then, of course, there were drinking games like Cardinal Puff, and chugging songs and challenges. It was a very learning atmosphere. The upperclassmen or instructors as we called them, were very dedicated as long as monthly checks from home came through.

About halfway through the second semester I was well bogged down in all-night b.s. sessions and cramming for an upcoming mid-term in general business when there was a knock at my dorm door.

"You must be James," said a blonde-haired, blue-eyed frat man when I opened the door. He was wearing traditional Midwestern Greek man attire: blue silk windbreaker with a large crest over his heart, bordered by Greek letters in script, signifying Sigma --. He had a white thread sweater over a blue shirt, tan cords, tennis shoes, and a fancy sapphire and diamond pin and chain attached to the sweater.

"Ah, yea that' me," I nearly stuttered, never having been this close to what surely must be the biggest ass-bandit I'd ever seen.

"My name is John Perkins. My father has some business dealings in Chicago and, through a friend, knows of your father. I told my Dad I'd stop over and see you. Welcome to old B.U."

I wiped my hand and shook his, trying to be as cool as possible.

"I know you didn't go through fall rush, James, and I wanted to stop by and see why. I mean, I can take one look and see you're Greek material. You're a business major, aren't you?"

"That's right. I was just studying for a midterm. I've got my first one in General Business in two days."

"Who's your instructor, Dr. Brown?"

"Yea, that's right," I said. I'd been thinking about pledging a house but figured I'd wait until sophomore year. Maybe my complexion would clear up by then. I knew I'd have to be in a house to make it to any of the parties. The GDI or goddamn independent life consisted of going to a movie in downtown Peoria, followed by a pizza (zero high school – ought).

"Listen, James," Perkins said, looking behind him, and then closing the door. "We've got a guy in the house who's one of Brown's assistants in another course. Grab a jacket and we'll go over to the house and see him."

I had sort of waited until the last moment and there were still two chapters I hadn't read. I figured I had nothing to lose.

John hit me with the full history of the "house" in 12 minutes flat as we walked across the quad.

"I don't know if you know this," he began as I struggled to keep up with him, "but we've been the number one house on campus scholastically for three out of the last four semesters. Our pledges were first the last two semesters in a row. You'll probably notice a lot of trophies in the living room.

"We were also first last year in intramural baseball, second in touch football and track and third in basketball. Two of our big boys had the flu during the play-offs."

Soon we were walking down a street known as fraternity row, even though I could see some were sorority houses. I could smell the remnants of spaghetti, meatloaf, even bar-b-q steaks and baked pies. I heard high-pitched screaming and saw that a co-ed water balloon fight appeared to be nearing conclusion. Then it was all a blur of introductions.

"Brother Hughes, this is James. Brother Harrison, brother Thompson, brother Miller, and on and on. Large speakers blared Ray Charles Greatest Hits.

Finally we went downstairs where Perkins and brother Plumly got a key and opened the door to the File Room. It was more of a large walk-in closet packed with file cabinets from floor to ceiling. Perkins opened a drawer marked "General Business," and pulled out a large manila folder marked "Brown."

"Well, here's all the tests he's given during the last three years," Perkins said matter-of-factly. "They're all pretty much the same...multiple choice. He just varies the questions."

He handed me five different tests marked "Intro. To Bus. 2nd semester mid-term exam." All I could do was whistle.

"We'll take them upstairs to my room and you can study them for a while...but these never leave the house. Do you understand!" I tried to nod yes with the respect one gives to the Catholic church.

The House itself was an old, wooden three-story structure, the kind my mother would call a firetrap. But I was impressed by the wood paneling, the highly polished banister (how rough could pledge work actually be?) and the comforting aroma of cologne, pipe tobacco and coffee.

Almost every inch of wall space downstairs was taken up by paddles, photos of the original founders, group shots of the brothers over the years, trophies, certificates of merit and engraved crests. Rooms upstairs, of course, were plastered with playboy centerfolds, and snapshots with captions like, "super lay," "one night stand," or "three weeks and counting."

I was introduced to Brother Richards – another solid WASP who appeared to be diligently copying a term paper submitted by a graduate student at the U. of Illinois.

"This guy has to be the most long-winded son of a bitch I've ever seen," Richards muttered. "Two to one he got this shit from a Yalie. Probably a rich kid from Scarsdale whose dad's a lawyer and had a client dig up the background. It's like I'm going to have to go straight from the introduction to the conclusion to make it short enough. At least the graphs are footnoted."

"Ok. Hold it down," Perkins said, picking up the recent Playboy. "James has gotta study for a test in Brown's business class. Then we're going out for a couple of beers."

More than 100 students were enrolled in Brown's Introduction to Business class. We sat in every other seat of a small auditorium as assistants passed out the tests. I took one look and knew I had it made. It was hard not to break out smiling. Particularly when I noticed the guy next to me had definitions written on both arms, from his wrists to his elbows. He was casually pulling the sleeves of his sweater up and down. Zero high school trick. Ought.

The grades were posted two days later on the bulletin board outside Brown's office, about two hours after I agreed to pledge Sigma – the next semester. Fourteen persons, including myself, had gotten a 95 or better. Then the grades fell back to a range of from 76 to 21. There were no B's and only 45 C's. But Brown showed his true colors the next day.

"Good morning class," he said. "As you can tell by the grades on the midterm exam, we've got a few real smart students in the class. And strangely enough, most of them are fraternity men. To offset this fact, I've decided to make a few changes in my grading method this semester.

"First, we will have three more tests including the final, and I am going to drop your lowest test score before computing your final grade. Secondly, I've placed in the reserve section of the library, copies of all the tests I've given in this course during the last few years.

"You will now all have a chance to study previous tests. Fifty percent of the questions on the remaining exams will be taken from these tests. The answers, of course, will not necessarily be the same, due to different wording.

"And while you're at the library, also in the reserve section, you will find a number of books I've selected for outside reading material. Assistants will now pass out a list of chapters in these books which I want you to read. Fifty percent of the questions on the remaining tests will cover material in these reading assignments."

His voice droned on and I slouched back in my seat. Luckily, however, my score on the first test held me up pretty well. I ended up with a B in the course.

I pledged the fraternity the next semester and it was no big deal: running errands, trying to remember all the Brothers names and hometowns, chugging beers, singing old Sigma – songs. Then, of course, there were special songs for special occasions. Most of them, our chapter president had declared, were not to be sung in public, like "Human Relations:"

> You with your swinging noses,
> Come join the league of Moses,
> Fight! Fight! Fight for Palestine.
> You with your beans and gravy,
> Come join the Yiddish navy,
> Fight! Fight! Fight for Palestine.

You-ou who pinch the penny,
We love you most of any
"Fight! Fight! Fight for Palestine.
Isaac, Able, Jacob, Sam
We're the boys who eat no ham.
Schickels, schackels, clutch them tight.

Synagogue Synagogue, Fight! Fight!
Fight!

So I did my little chores around the house, even though I was
still living in a dorm. Pushups and blind dates. The pledge walk-out
where we captured two Brothers and took them for the weekend to
another chapter in another state. There was nothing like forty of us
or more in a bar on a Friday night, half smashed and singing to liven
the place up:

High above a Pi Phi's garter
High above her knee.
There's a bit of Pi Phi passion
waiting there for me.
Lift her skirt, oh lift it gently,
lay her in the grass.
What I wouldn't give for
just a piece of Pi Phi ass.

Finally one day after hell week I was blindfolded, went
through the ritual and was a Brother. But all I really remember
of my sophomore year, 1963, was that unforgettable day crowded
around the television after Kennedy was shot. The rest is pretty
much a blur of beer and cramming for tests.

I was, to be honest, still a virgin except for touching. And
my standards weren't all that high, either. Like I always asked. I
never refused. After drinking for two hours on a Friday, I'd call a

girl's dorm pay phone and say I needed a blind date for a very shy but handsome fraternity boy. It wasn't difficult to find some GDI who hadn't had a date all year to say yes.

My goal was to line up two or three dates, about ten minutes apart. Then I'd sit in the lobby of the girls' dorm reading a paper. If the chick had any possibilities, like large breasts but under 130 pounds, I'd identify myself. If not, I'd say, "oh, you must have the wrong person. I have a date."

I would usually end up with the kind of girl one never takes out in public, so we'd buy a couple of six-packs and hustle over to the old Sugar Shack apartment rented by the frat house so brothers would have a place to legally party on weekends. It probably goes without saying my famous plan never worked because I'd usually be too drunk to care anyway. I mean I didn't want to get hooked into getting married.

Of course taking a chick back to the dorm at 12:45 a.m. is a different matter. The last fifteen mutes before girls' hours are up is one frantic scene: sixty or more couples: half of them making out to impress others, the other half shaking hands and checking out other people to see whom they're with.

Since one can't help but be recognized under the spotlights, my favorite line was to convince the girl that it would be super-cool to pretend we just got back from a masquerade party, or that we wished to remain anonymous just to blow everyone else's minds.

It sounds rather absurd sober, but when half crocked, success can be relatively assured. I'd just grab a couple of paper bags, cut eye and mouth holes in them, and slip them over our heads. The only loophole in the plan, I found, was showing up in my white MGB which I always managed to drive up on the sidewalk, usually right through the crowd and up to the front door.

Invariably, some guy, usually a true-blue fraternity brother with his pin mate, would recognize me by my car and shout out my name at the top of his lungs. Then I'd have to drive off before someone could grab the bag off my head, confirming his suspicion.

But if I made a clean get-away, one could never be positive it was me: Me? Come on, brother Hughes. Would I have the guts to do something like that? Of course I don't want to give the house a bad name. I did loan my car to a friend last night, though. Wait until I find that bastard.

****

It's junior year and I've moved out of the frat house, changed my major to English and Philosophy and spend my spare time reading Kant, Kierkegaard and Sartre. I just don't think I have much in common with the lifestyle and prejudices of any of the brothers. But I still show up a couple of times a month so I can pay dues and attend any good parties.

I have two roommates including one who is also a drop-out brother and we've rented the top half of a mansion style, three-story house overlooking downtown Peoria. My other roommate, Jerry, studies almost every waking moment, determined to get straight A's and readmission to Northwestern University.

Besides cramming and alcohol abstinence, I find out Jerry has one exception to his good boy image: once every few weeks he allows himself the reward of visiting his personal hooker downtown in the notorious Aiken Alley district.

"I'll give you a couple of bucks for driving me downtown," Jerry said last night. After a little more prodding and a reassurance that there was no chance the place could be busted while we were there, we headed out.

Jerry told me he'd known his present woman for two months, and was dutifully loyal to her to the tune of twenty bucks. She was, he said, very new at the trade. In fact, he said he met her on the second day she'd been working there and she was so inexperienced she kept worrying about the fact that she was always climaxing. He said she had recently gotten over the problem except, of course, when he came for his Friday night session.

We parked a few blocks away: I didn't want to pull up to the door in my car with college stickers all over it. Along the street, however, I noticed several other cars with Bradley stickers in the back windows and a few with fraternity letters. I checked out one and it said TKE, naturally, since they were the football jock house.

We went up to a door which had a mirror facing out, Jerry knocked and we were promptly hustled in by a fat cab driver with a cigar in his mouth. Somehow I had expected something somewhat flashier. Then too, I was slightly grossed-out by the madam who, by way of introduction, promptly frisked us, her hand grabbing me a little too hard between the legs, causing me to yelp and her to produce a husky laugh that developed into a cough and ended when she spit a wad of phlegm into the sink.

I was told that Jerry usually stayed with his girl for an extra long time, so I excused myself and went outside with the intention of stealing one of the Aiken Alley street signs for a wall decoration. I finally removed it and got it to the car but not before slicing my hand pretty good.

They bandaged me up back in the brothel where I spent another 45 minutes fighting off the advances of the two remaining hookers who looked to be well in their thirties and could have used a little weight loss exercises in their hips.

Candy

> The face of Candy – tight, sensual,
> expressive, ageless, gentle wet lips
> that perk like a child of six.
> Medium-full breasts; sensitive, soft,
> straight-matched legs, thin, firm calves.
> A hole in the seat of her shorts
> and no underwear: I love her.

The most wonderful, beautiful time I had in those three years was with a young girl I met at a movie theater. We dated for two weeks until her parents found out, leading me to do research on how to change my name.

There is no way to describe in words making love on a blanket covering wet grass when suddenly the brightest light in the world shines upon you, the ground begins to shake and you realize you are only ten feet from railroad tracks and it's too late to move.

Covering her, I looked up just in time to see both engineers gawking out the same window with giant smiles on their faces as they blew the train whistle. To this day I will swear there must have been well over two hundred boxcars on that train.

The Ass Man

I both knew her and I loved her,
the moment that we met.
I was trapped, knew it hopeless,
yet I couldn't find regret.
We were lovers on the first night,
we held hands on the third;
My lips brushed hers with pleasure
'till she trembled as a bird.
But as the months passed slowly,
as we knew each other's mind,
I felt suddenly with coldness,
it was like the gears that grind.
There was no feeling sorry,
No long involved adieu.
I simply took her diamonds
and made it to Peru.

I cannot deny my biggest mistake came one night in late spring when I had another dormitory blind date and, as usual, I didn't have sex but compensated for this fact by consuming straight shots in addition to an unknown number of beers.

My date was easily convinced to go along with the old paper bags over our heads routine. But, as it turned out, she loved the idea so much she began screaming with laughter and we soon had a crowd around us cheering us on. Before I knew it I had driven up the three steps to the double door entranceway, and, with the doors held wide open, I felt I had no choice but to drive right in to the lobby.

I backed out quickly, of course, probably leaving rubber marks, but I swear I never took the paper bag off my head.

I tried for nearly an hour to convince the Dean of Men that I had loaned my car out that night and there was no proof it was me. I certainly wasn't able to produce the real culprit because it wouldn't be right for me to rat on him. All to no avail.

Somehow I was allowed to finish the remaining two weeks of school and my finals, but I was to be suspended for the full next fall semester to give me time to decide what I wanted to do with my life.

I tried to study those next two weeks but I knew it was hopeless. I even started hanging around the fraternity house again, trying to see if I could get a little help in preparation for finals and maybe even a little sympathy.

And so, as the boys threw another log upon the fire that last week in May, 1965, twenty or so men sat in the living room humming, singing a few songs. And I reflected upon my three college years in the dear old halls of ivy: super basketball school, I'm going to miss you, I thought.

The brothers sang the Sigma – sweetheart song. Then they even sang a song they had rehearsed just for me:

Friends may come
and friends may go.
Friends may peter out, you know.
But we'll be yours
through thick or thin.
Peter out, or peter in.

The Summer of 1965

That summer I was plagued by the what-to-now syndrome. I wandered about the house aimlessly. I bought about my third record ever and kept playing the same songs over and over: "I want to hold your hand..." and "I've just met a girl today..." What was there to say? What was there left for me in life?

I rummaged through my small belongings, from basement to attic. The toy soldiers and the Lionel train set. I read poetry. Herman Hess. The Prophet by Kahil Gibran. I thought of a major in existential dualism and metaphysical phenomenon ology.

A Rainy Saturday

The things I saw today
in the third floor walk-up storage room
may not halt a war
or make a nation stop and think.
Few, in fact, will even gaze upon these printed forms.
But on those long-forgotten musty boards,
laid in earlier years
by damp-stained rags and yellow pages,
some human forms had hoarded and saved
a hundred items they thought might once again
please the eye or mind.
I cannot say what their spot in creation,
or what to replace today.
Yet these items held my thoughts
for a dozen hours or more.
And even now, when all have been discarded,
from time to time I wonder
what memories they might have meant
for some other poor soul.
But who was I to judge their worth?

James

The Army would grab me now. I wouldn't be stationed in Germany and work as a spy. Only Vietnam, rice paddies and death. Hadn't I seen it on the six o'clock news? I might as well be picking out a gravesite now.

But no, not death. Surely not me. Perhaps the loss of an arm (the one-armed detective in a large city, tough, brutal, getting back at the world and making it with women, driving a Ferrari insanely fast). Or maybe I'd lose a leg (wearing a wooden leg, using a cane to fight, becoming a famous correspondent). Or perhaps even an eye: I even practiced before the mirror. (Yes, that's it, the one-eyed gambling, boozing, brawling, balling hero. Idol to thousands, legend in my own time). Anything. But no way was I going to be zapped.

Then one afternoon I was sitting at a bar near my parents' house that didn't particularly check ids if they knew you were going to college, when I saw an old high school classmate.

"Hey, Chris," I said. "Haven't seen you in three years. What've you been doing?"

"Well, what do you know, James," he said in his deep, even voice. He looked about 28 and always had a somewhat condescending manner. And who did he think he was, anyway? He was wearing a tweed jacket over a button down shirt. And a tie. In 90 degree weather. I knew he didn't get good enough grades for his father to have gotten him into an ivy league school.

"I put in three years at Bradley," I said. "But I'm temporarily suspended for a semester. You know. I was living a bit too wild and I got caught. But what about you?"

"Well, I went to the University of Illinois for a year, but I've been going to a small college in Colorado. You wouldn't believe it. Classes in the morning and evenings. Ski all day. No one, including the teachers, goes to class if the powder is good. Why don't you come out and try it?"

"Yea, it sounds good, but shit. It's the middle of August already. I'd never get accepted this late."

"Are you kidding," he said. "They accept anyone. There were

It is the Fall

only about 60 students last year, but they're trying to get as many as they can. Come over to my house tomorrow and we'll call the dean of admissions. He's a good friend, so it's no problem."

I was in heaven, my eyes in a trance as I watched him help a busty blonde into her sweater. He didn't even introduce me, but what the heck. I was going back to school. Did I care?

"Ok. Ok," I yelled after him. Did he hear me? I ran to the door as he was going out. "Be over at 10. All right? All right?"

He didn't answer. He just waved his hand to me over his shoulder and started whispering into the blonde's ear. She was a little heavy in the butt anyway.

"Another beer," I yelled to the bartender." I was smiles, all smiles, man. No war. No death. I was back in school.

And it all worked out fine. Chris called the dean who said I was tentatively accepted, pending two letters of recommendation. Our minister and my dad's lawyer came through in a flash. The letters were in the mail the following day.

Of course my parents weren't too impressed by the name: Yampa Valley College, Steamboat Springs, Colorado. Founded in 1962. Liberal Arts, enrollment 65, class C accreditation. Would another college accept their credits so I could graduate from a school at least worth mentioning down the road?

All minor hassles, I reminded them. I was going back to school and the Army wouldn't get me. Besides, I would get straight A's, and return to another school all the better for the experience.

Chris convinced me to put two fat blue racing stripes down the length of my white MGB. He had fake racing stripes down the length of his Alpha Romero. I thought putting numbers on the doors might be pushing it a little too far.

Before I knew it, there we were racing across the plains states heading for the Rocky Mountains. I like to believe that at the time few cars had made it faster on the road from Chicago to Denver. This was due less to the fact that racing stripes add 10 miles per hour to the speed that a vehicle will drive than to our adherence to the creed that no car would pass us and we would pass everything in sight.

I remember pulling into small town gas stations in Iowa and Kansas, screeching to a halt, bounding out of our cars, grabbing the pumps ourselves and yelling at each other as we checked our oil and gave the windows a quick wiping.

The attendants had a habit of running around and yelling, "What's going on here? Who do you think you are?"

"Cross country race," we'd yell back. "5,000 dollars at stake. We're ahead. Fifty cars behind us!"

Then we'd peel off singles, rounding to the nearest dollar, and leave a patch of rubber as we squealed out of the station. In the rear view mirror the picture was always the same: the gas pump jockey standing in the street, watching us go up through the gears, then looking the other way to see if the other cars were coming yet.

It is the Fall

Colorado

I had seen the Rocky Mountains before, of course, but to stay at the Broadmoor in Colorado Springs at age ten or to drive an MG with the top down through canyons west of Boulder is one trip that separates the passenger from the pilot.

It was a warm, early September afternoon, a Beatles song was blaring and the smells, the colors and the blue sky were truly in tune. On we flew, past boulders and clay and granite, near cold canyon streams, through echoing tunnels, past sheer cliffs of crumbling, sliding stone. Honking past early autumn mountain hay fields and their Colorado beef with big, dumb eyes staring, 300 strong, watching us slide by. Highway 40 all the way...Berthoud Pass, be ready.

Chris in the lead, his Alpha hanging around corners (come on. Try to lose me. Big chance of that – ought). Singing, no screaming, to the squeals of tires, radio overpowering. The Beatles again? "I can't find the time or place where we just met she's just the girl for me and I want all the world to see she's mine..." Sweet freedom and youth. How I love you! Orange and yellow, bronze and brown, olive and green-green colors bursting and I one with all. I was alive!

Up, up we drove. Up "S" shaped roads, through patches of pine scent and aspen. Then down, passing on rock-banked curves, sliding on loose pebbles, fresh cold air, then heart pumping blood, wiping sweaty palms. There was no stopping our streaking, frantic pace, like the Pike's Peak scramblers we thought we were.

"I care. I care," I yelled at no one out into the air. "I love my life!" Sweet blue-striped, after-burning, Denver-installed new straight-pipe wailing, deep hollow echoes trailing, bouncing back off rock walls.

Two hours later we paused on the lower part of Rabbit Ears Pass, then pulled over and climbed out of our cars. Below us was an incredibly beautiful, golden valley, five miles wide and twenty miles long.

"There she is," Chris said. "Home."

Ten minutes later we were revving up our engines as we made a slow pass through the storefront town of Steamboat Springs. Past four motels, three gas stations, three clothing stores, two ski shops, a Laundromat, bank, hardware store, three bars and some gurgling and sulfur smelling springs and that's that. Twelve blocks of main street.

"What?" I kept yelling as I tail-gated Chris. "What the hell is this?" The college, man, I thought. "Where the hell's the college?" I yelled as I pulled alongside him.

"Relax," he said. "Let's get a beer."

Then Chris, old buddy, filled me in on the "little details" he forgot to mention. Like the fact that there were no real classrooms or dormitories.

"Actually," he related with a smile, "there really isn't a campus, as yet. But it's all planned. They're going to start work on the first buildings next spring. Just as soon as they come up with the money."

"Well, who is this 'they' you keep referring to?" I said.

"Oh, there's Mrs. Bogue, founder of the school and, of course, the board of trustees. You, know, people who put up the money to hire teachers and get the thing moving. Like a half dozen or so townspeople. There's the guy who runs the drugstore, another owns a clothing store and I guess a couple of bankers. Most of them are pretty good people, although I would say they're a bit conservative. The whole thing is pretty experimental. Very informal."

"But where are the classes held?"

"The school rents about six houses in town, where some of the students will be staying and some of the classes are held there. A few are held in one of the churches, and then there's the cafeteria downtown where we'll all eat this year. What difference does it make where they're held, anyway?"

"I'm just trying to get the feel of things," I said. "I think I'll get another beer."

"Yea. You'll be doing a lot of drinking here. That's about all there is to do around here – besides skiing."

"There are two 3.2 beer bars in town, but one, the Pioneer, is strictly a cowboy bar. Last spring they used to stand out in front of it on weekends to pick fights with college kids. I heard it wasn't long ago that a bunch of cowboys got drunk one Saturday night and they almost hung some Indian. Luckily the town cop – there's only one on duty at a time – walked in just as they were throwing a rope over a rafter."

"You've got to be kidding?"

"No, it's the truth. It's still legal to wear a gun at your side in town, if it's not concealed. And wait until hunting season. Hunters come from all over the country right to this town. Big, self-contained rigs, pulling a jeep, which is pulling two snowmobiles. But you'll see. You'll love it. The powder snow makes for the best skiing in the U.S."

I wouldn't be honest if I didn't say I was pretty mad at Chris for the next couple of days. In fact, if it wasn't for the fact that the college was going to keep me out of the Army, I might not have begun unpacking my bags.

I got a map of Routt County and spent the next week driving on gravel roads, trying not to bottom out. I drove to the back of Strawberry Park behind town and up a winding road to the Hot Springs. I looked down over the town from above Fairview on the top of Blackmare drive. Then to the top of Buffalo Pass and finally north of town all the way to Hahn's Peak.

The colors of the Aspen had not yet turned to yellow and flaming orange and red, but the scrub oak were already a deep Indian red.

What I couldn't believe was the lack of anything at the base of the ski area. There was only an A-frame building and a restaurant and a couple of old buildings and a chairlift. Land, I was told, is going for $5,000 to $10,000 an acre at the base of the ski area, but a little higher along a road that circles above the base because it is more desirable to be able to look down on a ski resort.

The biggest surprise came when students started rolling into town the next week. Suddenly it was no longer a hick, mountain cowboy town in the middle of nowhere. New students were driving out of place vehicles with license plates from New York and California. It took about a week to discuss whose father was president of what company and how much each girl was supposed to be worth. There were little cliques for the first few weeks, then the whole school, all 80 or so of us, seemed pretty much one big, happy crowd.

The teachers were actually quite good and I particularly enjoyed a course in international relations from an instructor who served in the Diplomatic Service. Students were staying in two rented houses on the corner of 5th and Pine and seven cottages at 8th and Pine known as the men's village. I opted for a private room, as did 10 others, at the Harbor Hotel, which was fine except on Saturday nights when there was a downstairs band next door.

Chris had told me that the year before there had been a small college paper so I went to the local newspaper, The Pilot, and cut a deal to have a paper printed twice a month. It was an old hot lead press where letters were set by hand, and melted down again at the end of the week. I got Paul and Jim who were students from L.A. to hustle $5.00 to $10.00 ads per issue from 20 merchants in town and put out the Talisman newspaper twice a month.

Aspen

One Friday morning, around the last week of October, I woke up and suddenly was obsessed with the thought that I had to see Aspen. I knew it was only about a three hour drive or maybe a little longer depending on road conditions.

It had been snowing on and off for several weeks, but the roads were basically dry. I hurriedly packed two bags because I've never traveled light in my life. I grabbed a map, two six packs and without telling anyone, I was out the door.

I headed east on Highway 40, then turned right on 131, driving through Oak Creek and on to Wolcott where I turned right heading toward Glenwood Springs. I couldn't believe the steep granite canyons before Glenwood where I had read that some of the best climbers in the country had learned their skills with rope and pitons.

The last 40 miles to Aspen is a winding two lane highway with plenty of drop-offs. It is considered one of the more treacherous roads in the country during a blinding snowstorm. It was nearly dark by 4 p.m. but I was able to get a room at an old rundown building called the Hotel Jerome for under $30.

After checking in, I went down to the bar and was greeted by the most electric, magical atmosphere I've ever experienced in my life. The place was packed with ski instructors and ski patrolmen, male and female, most of whom had already been taking classes on Aspen Mountain even though it didn't open until Thanksgiving.

It was like something out of a movie. People were speaking with French, German and British accents, vibrant with high-altitude red sunburned faces, raccoon-like in appearance from goggles which were worn around necks or high up on the arms. And everyone, I mean everyone, was like the most beautiful and athletic people I've ever seen. The women's suspenders only seemed to exemplify their perfect, full breasts which were dying to jump out of their sweaters.

The air was almost stifling. Everyone was yelling, certainly all talking at the same time. And every time the door opened, people cheered and greeted a newcomer like a long lost friend. Some of the instructors must have been at least 35. Did they actually make a living just skiing? And getting paid for it at the same time? I mean what a way to make a living.

I had no one to talk with. I must have looked like an albino. All I could do was stand in the corner and stare. Finally I decided to take a walk, stepped outside and was slapped in the face by cold air from the nearly 8,000 feet of elevation.

I walked down the street and was enthralled by the smells of cooking steaks, hamburgers, French fries and wood smoke. Every building seemed to have smoke coming out of its chimney.

I looked up and millions of snowflakes were falling down from the stars. It was like I was on another planet. Surely no other place in the entire world could be as special and surreal as this. It was like a dream. I never wanted to wake up. And I knew I would always have to come back to something like this. It was as though my life was just beginning.

When I was back outside the bar I casually joined a circle of people standing near an alley and was invited to try pot for the first time in my life. I didn't really feel a thing. But maybe it was because of the booze I was drinking.

It is the Fall

My First Trip

There was another student staying at the Harbor Hotel named Doug who looked totally emaciated with his reddish hair and pale complexion. He usually wore a stocking cap and ultra-dark shades. He never spoke to anyone, so I began to single him out, trying to figure out his background.

Soon we were chatting a bit, and I learned that he had been suspended for a semester from Yale, due to illness and he decided to come to Colorado to go to school "to get his head straight" as he put it. He later said he broke his leg cracking up a motorcycle and was caught with a pound of pot in his backpack. But the thought of the phrase "getting his head straight" still brings a smile to my face.

I admired Doug for how well read he was in Greek literature and philosophy. Especially existentialism: "Uh...essentially, uh... 'man's awareness of his illogical position in a meaningless world.' I believe that would be the most succinct definition." His one idol in life, however, was Bob Dylan.

I think the key to our friendship began when I mentioned that I had tried grass for the first time the previous weekend while in Aspen.

"Weed, man? Pot? Boo? Hemp? You dig it? Tremendous. Groovy. Tell me immediately, what did you feel? Perceptions, man. What? What? What?"

"It's hard to explain," I said. "I mean I didn't really feel anything."

"Nothing? Come on, James. You must have felt something... ahh, your first time. Nothing? Yes, you didn't even know what to look for. But the other people, what did they do?"

"Well, they just...uh...nothing really. They just sort of stood around saying, "'Wow, man. Too much.'"

Doug chuckled. "Yes, I guess they would. Well, have no fear. A friend of mine is sending some out and it should be here shortly. I feel certain you will have some sort of perceptual sensation. Rest assured."

Then he broke into his long, low chuckle again and looked at me with his yellow-brown, wandering eyes.

Doug's boo did arrive in a few days and I can safely say that by the end of the week I was thoroughly initiated into the club. All the while I was forced to describe my sensations, perceptions and thoughts. And Doug kept playing the same Bob Dylan record over and over again evaluating every word like it was something from the Bible, for Christ sake.

I never had any bad effects, although I occasionally found myself feeling a bit guilty: I was, after all, a lawbreaker. I also found it necessary to purchase a pair of dark sunglasses to cut down on the glare during the day and to ward off feelings that straight waitresses might somehow look into my eyes and be able to tell I was stoned.

Doug was not the coolest guy in the world, however. It wasn't long before we had met a couple of townies, one of them trying to get divorced, and we were doing heavy make-out sessions in the back of their car. Doug, of course, had to smoke right in front of them, completely disregarding the fact that they were likely to tell someone. I was soon having my first feelings of what he described as "meaningless paranoia." But, Doug's total confidence in the belief that we would remain undiscovered enabled me to "keep my cool."

There is a Friday that I remember very well. I was quietly sipping a beer at the Pioneer 3.2 bar which now gladly served students, and matching the bartender for the juke box, when Doug walked in. He was happier than I'd ever seen him before.

"James, baby, ohhh. Come here," he began, as he edged me around the corner of the bar. He was squealing and I tried to calm him, hoping one of the derelicts at the bar wouldn't take him for a fag.

"It's here, baby. It's here," he said in a stage whisper. "Look." Good old Doug unwrapped a small piece of tinfoil, exposing a one inch square of blue litmus paper.

"What is it?"

"Acid, man. LSD. It just arrived in the mail. It's the Leary shit and my sister got it at Radcliffe. And I'm going to take some. It's great, man. You'll love it."

"I don't think so," I said. "Grass, yea. But I don't want to get into that heavy shit."

"Oh, James, you have to. I mean that's what I got it for. It's great. You'll love it. Really."

"No, I don't know. I mean look...I gotta take a piss. Be right back." My palms were sweating. I went into the john and looked at myself in the mirror. My eyes were lit up. Contact high, I thought. I went back to the bar and saw Doug sipping a beer. Contemplating.

"Look, man," he said, "there's nothing habit-forming or narcotic about it. I know dozens of people who've dropped back East. No problem. No hangover. I've done it myself several times. It's essentially a stimulant to perceptual faculties. Great to make love on. Let's call those townies and we'll go to Aspen and get a motel room."

I took another sip of beer. I couldn't think of a reason why I shouldn't. I'd never read anything about it the papers, except a couple of items about Leary and his experiments and how it was considered on the top of the list for new kicks.

"I just don't know. I'll have to think about it."

"Well it's too late now," he said. "I put some in your beer while you were gone."

"You're kidding!" A sudden pang of emptiness went through my stomach. My heart was palpitating. How could he? I didn't see it floating.

"Did you really? You asshole! You bastard! I said I wasn't sure."

"Let's go. We don't have much time," he said. Then he was at the phone calling the girls.

I sat at the bar, shocked. I ordered another beer. My best friend, I thought. A real bastard.

"It's all set," he said. "Hurry up. We've gotta move fast. You won't even need a toothbrush."

I couldn't believe it. I was stoned on acid and on my way back to Aspen. I had a test on Monday and a paper due. Doug helped me out the door. I was almost stumbling.

We walked the three blocks to the girls' house. They were all excited about the trip. Twenty years in this town and they hadn't even been to Aspen yet, a three-hour drive away. The two of them had filled a mother-may-I giant size suitcase which must have weighed seventy pounds. Doug grabbed it and struggled to the car with it. He was cackling with pleasure and suddenly very gallant. And I was getting more stoned.

But I wasn't stoned yet. Doug informed me after we'd been on the road for about an hour that he had just been kidding.

"You don't put this in someone's food, man," he said. "I mean you could blow their mind. One has to want to take it. Like me."

He then divided the precious paper into eight parts, swallowed a piece and handed another to me. He hadn't put it in my beer after all. Now I was obligated to take it, swallow the paper. I even licked my fingers to get the full benefit. Jane did the same but Betty was driving.

"Maybe we can even play switchies," Doug said, giggling.

"Yea, well you can forget that idea," Betty said. She must have been doing seventy. She's pissed because she has to drive, I thought. Well piss on her. She won't even know what she's doing when she's wasted, anyway.

An hour later (or was it less?) I suddenly began to notice how bleary the lights were becoming. It was past four and nearly dusk; we had just entered Glenwood Springs. Silver-blue circles shot out at me from car headlights, lamplights, colored neon signs – 30 feet in all directions. Colors were bouncing off everything. Turquoise, pea-green, orange-yellow, jade, pink, red, American blue.

"Jesus, you're speeding...I mean really recklessly. On the curves. Christ, Betty, slow down, will you?" Was I yelling?

It is the Fall

"Forty. I'm doing forty. The limit's fifty."

"On these corners? You're crazy. Look at the drop off!"

"James, baby. It's ok, man," Doug said. "Nothing...to worry about. Slow down a little...will you. He's right, god damit. Will you slow down?"

"That's better," I said. "Still...could do a little slower...I mean. JESUS. Did you see that? That guy who just passed us... must have been doing eighty. On these roads? He's crazy."

My head was spinning. Snowflakes were now shooting past the car like stars. I couldn't see more than ten feet in front of the car.

"Better slow down, Betty," Doug said. "Be careful, baby... really snowing out there."

"I'm doing fifteen miles an hour in a 50 zone," she yelled back. "We'll get arrested if we go any slower. Why don't you all just shut up and let me drive?"

Doug turned on the radio. The snowflakes were soaring past the windshield, darting up or sideways at the last moment. Like meteorites passing a spaceship at the speed of light. And leaving tiny trails where they had been. White coming out of the blue. Out of the black. Hypnotizing. Frantic. Oh, ecstatic wonder. Secrets revealed at last!

Then a sign: Aspen. Then over a bridge and we drove into town. Betty hadn't taken her acid. The only straight one. The only sane one. (She saved us) But Doug gave her what we all had taken and spoke as evenly as he could muster.

"Any cost, man. Just get it...double beds...go."

She was out. The three of us alone in the car. Quiet. Getting colder. Snowing like crazy. Jane was moaning, "what's happening?" But neither Doug nor I could explain. I was so totally off, so stoned, so... "What's she doing? What's ...taking ...her...wow...relax..." I never wanted to be this high. Just a little, sure, but so spaced, so...

"Oh, I see it all now," I said. "I understand. So obvious. Just like...I always thought it...I was right...all along."

"Yea, baby," Doug said. "We're off. Really off."

"Oh, what's going on?" Jane cooed. "Oh. Hold me. Ohhh."

"James…I know…what you mean. It's …ah…grass… inferior…perceptually the …mental process…totally presented."

"Yes…but I can't quite…can't touch…it's not really…"

"yea, but…I know…but…"

Jane. Ah sweet Jane. Totally forgotten there for a second. Suddenly there. Alive with feeling. Response…yes…knowing…

"It's ok, honey. Just a little trip…just…good…I see." I was holding her, trying to show her awareness. Didn't need to. She saw.

Hours. No minutes later. Who knew? She was back. At last. Then we were parking, getting our stuff – their stuff – out of the car. We crept up the stairs, eyes in frantic-panic, like a cornered cat in a dark alley.

Finally. We were in the room: safe! Were we seen? No. No…aahhh. Laughing…on the floor, rolling over…tears from laughing…skin stretched…eyes beaming. And Betty starting to come on. The same amount? Yes, she took the same amount. But she isn't off yet. The store…food…sandwiches…money…cokes…a lot… of…different food…take ten…twenty…hurry. She'll be right back.

Laughing…my stomach…the mirror…hung up…hung up in the mirror. Eyes so perfect…face…perfect. Human. Fleshy. Realizing all…for the first time. Oohh…eyes reveal all. It's all there. Face…mouth…look at it. Smile…frown…cry. I can cry…look… for the first time…so long…I can cry. On demand. I CAN act! I'm beautiful. I'm hung-up. Oh…so sad, so non-loving. Never…I'll never go back…the same way. I CAN FEEL. Aahhh. Emotion. Sweet mirror. Scattered. Oh, my mind…just so scattered…

"I can't …think…"

"I know…baby…don't…fight…it. It's good…enjoy…oh, what good acid…oh, sister…beautiful…baby."

Back…she's back…food…now…laughing on the floor… LOUD…please…listen…frantic…eyes suddenly black…hollow… quiet…it's dead quiet…still. Listen. We were…too loud. Someone heard. They're coming...Who's coming? No...no one. No one heard...safe...we're safe.

"It's ok...shh. Ok...it's...shh...Doug brought us back. Ok... eat...shh!...laughing...quietly, shh...hmmm...mmm...mmhhmm... Oh...it's...good. Food...mmm...good...shh.

"OHHH! OHHH! HELP!"

Jane was screaming, jumping...on the bed...Shhh.

"Worms...Oh, God....worms...I ate worms...ohhh...in the sandwich."

"Nothing," Doug yelled, looking at the sandwich...opening it up on the floor with a coffee stirrer. "you...just imagined...hallucinated... stupid..."

"Let me see," I said. "Shut up...let...me see (was it possible?) Nothing. No...no...YES...there...look Doug...in mine too. In my hand." I hurled the sandwich on the floor.

"Yes," Doug said, stomping the barbeque beef sandwich into the rug. "But they're...not there...can't be...just imagined."

The mess...looks like blood. Italian beef sandwiches and bbq beef...blood and guts...human meat...ugh. The bed...move it over it...all of us...pushing it over...covered at last...gone.

It's ok. Laughing. All of us on the bed. Jane stepping on the chair, then the dressers.

"Don't step on the floor...the bible...throw it down...step on it...not the floor." Laughing. "Please...quiet."

The lights out. Sleep...can't...try...try...undress...off...take everything off. Each couple standing on beds, undressing.

"Heat...turn up the heat...bathroom...leave small light on..."

Bathroom...no, one at a time...no, all of us...standing there naked...no nude...nipples...breasts...Oh, look at them. I love them...beautiful...so soft. "No, don't touch." Aahh. Hair...dark black hair...more than me...than Doug. Mirror...laughing...smell... who's sweating...me...my hands...wet. Armpits...we're all looking at each other. Beautiful. Adam and Eve. To be...gods...to bed... warmer...touching.

Touching her breasts. Who? Joan? Jane? Barbara? Name?...
darling...ohh, touch...yes...my hand lost...inside her skin...inside
her breasts...darling...carol...fingers touching through the breasts...
oh my. Warmer. Still soft. Feet cold...kissing...stroking. Hours.
Where am I? Was I asleep? No. Still touching. Just tripping.

"I forgot. Doug. I forgot to make love. Ahh...how long...
when?"

"Shhh...hold it down...just...couple of minutes. Shhh.
Ahhh."

Doug's making it, I thought. I didn't have to say...he
understood...thoughts.

Jane was touching...kissing...harder...not fully, but...it's harder.
Don't kiss...in...put it in...almost, could be harder, but still...in...there.
There. Ahhh. It's in...I'm doing it...in Aspen. Good...I can feel...
so...prickly...warm...moving. It has me...I'm caught...pulling...there.
In and in...and out, out...slowly. Put it in...there...that's it...now faster.
Oh hurry...I'm going to...oh the colors...blue...flashing...traveling
through space...now...AAHHH...Oh, forever...so long...colors...
good...so beautiful...

Later. Lights on again. Eating more. More acid...yes. Not
quite as high, but high again. Then colors ...breasts...did I make
love again? No. Maybe. I don't think so...no matter. Sleep.
Finally sleep. At last.

It was noon. So tired, yet getting up. Four, maybe five
hours of sleep. But feeling strangely happy-rested – tired, yet full:
exhausted and satisfied. Breakfast, but couldn't eat. Then driving
back. Saturday. Going back to college. Having a few puffs of grass
on the way.

Sun glasses – man's greatest invention. Going back: the
same? But what an experience. Everything once for experience.
Eyes still stoned. Be better tomorrow. But the same? "For sure,"
Doug said. I believed him. I believed in him.

****

In December before Christmas Doug and I took the train from Steamboat to Denver, then booked a compartment on the train to Chicago where he continued on to New York City. We must have gone through about a dozen tunnels on the trip to Denver. It has to be one of the most beautiful views of the Rocky Mountains I've ever experienced.

We weren't far out of Steamboat when the train stopped at a station and someone came on board and took our orders for lunch. But then we pulled out of the station. About an hour later, at another station, someone came on board and began yelling, "Who's got the ham and cheese? Who's got the egg salad?"

I flew back after Christmas and got into skiing more seriously. If there was deep powder in the morning several classes changed the meeting schedule to late afternoon or evening. I was amazed at how well some of the students, particularly the locals who were raised in town, could ski.

On the weekends there might be a few National Ski Patrolmen, but during the week, if someone got injured, volunteers would just grab a toboggan lying near the top of the lifts, and give the hurt skier a fast, bumpy ride down the slopes. Some days the powder was so deep we had to wear a scarf over our noses and mouths to breathe.

Good old Doug never came back after Christmas, but it was about this time that I became fairly tight with a guy I'll call Robert who was from Massachusetts, and who was one of the better skiers, at least in terms of form. Coming from a divorced family, but with old school money, he had attended prep school in Switzerland and had a unique style of leaning way out over his skis, but with his skis so tight together they never separate.

Robert tried to teach me little tricks like either turning on top of moguls or bouncing off the sides in a turn to slow speed on steep slopes. It took me weeks to learn a tip roll when coming to a stop. But popping up on the ski tips just as I made a complete stop and changing direction 180 degrees was as close to a valid hot-dogger as I was ever going to get.

Robert also played the electric guitar quite well, but like many students with musical ability, he was better at jamming than actually putting memorized sets together and forming a polished, money-making band.

I soon learned that Robert always had his own, never-ending stash of weed, and for his whole life, as long as I knew him, he loved to have two hits of pot first thing in the morning: "Hey, it's no fun getting up in the morning knowing that's as high as you're going to be all day" was his motto. 8:30 am with first class at 9 am. No problem. Two tokes of pot with his shortened hash pipe.

Robert scored long wooden pipes with brass on each end in various Chinatowns, then cut the wood down to make the whole rig about five or six inches long. I think there was always a pipe clipped to the visor in his car.

After a while I found myself way too paranoid to even think about going to class or out in public stoned. The peer pressure of Robert trying to get me to have "just one little hit" became a never-ending obsession of his during our relationship.

On rare occasions, like on some of the first spring days of the year, Robert and I would drive out on Highway 40, then head toward Oak Creek, where we'd pull over and watch the cattle. If you yelled or mooed loud enough, sometimes the whole herd would come trotting over to the fence and stand there bellowing while the two of us yelled out the window at them.

That Summer

The summer of 1966 Robert invited me to visit him at his uncle's home near Woods Hole, Mass. He drove me around Falmouth, Nantucket and Martha's Vineyard where I had read new singers like Carly Simon and James Taylor were bunked in at glorious estates adding their messages to the unlikely fame of the Beatles. What I didn't know was that by the time I got there in late July, Robert had found a more potent friend and companion: Pure crystal meth.

Shortly after our drive began, he encouraged and badgered me into trying just a few lines of the stuff. And, of course, they were not small lines. Within a few minutes I was higher than I'd ever been or wanted to be. About all I could do was chain-smoke cigarettes and demand beers and a couple of drinks in a futile attempt to come down and return to my former self.

We drove through some quaint little towns and on one block I saw three restaurants which each had signs reading, "World's Best Clam Chowder."

All the houses in the areas we drove by were 3-story monsters and Robert finally pulled into the driveway of a home where he said his dealer lived. The two of them began talking rapid-fire in stage whispers too intertwined to be understood. Apparently a friend, whose parents were away for two weeks but who actually owned the house, was literally holed up in the basement where he had been getting high for three days straight.

There was a long, winding wooden stairway to the basement and I noticed a hole dug in the dirt floor about the exact size for a casket. A dozen mirrors of various size and age surrounded the pit, all seeming to direct the sunlight from three windows into the hole. The three of us walked to the edge and stared in amazement at the thin, gaunt, longhaired figure lying in the hole, naked except for boxer underwear.

His hands were folded across his chest and a large presumably

James   49

glass ring on the middle finger of his right hand seemed to reflect the sunlight off the mirrors.

"John. John," Robert's friend repeated. No answer.

"He's been like this for about two and a half days. He said when he gets up, he'll have all the power of the universe harnessed in that ring and he'll be able to walk down the street and zap anyone who is not bringing positive feelings to this planet. Hasn't eaten either. We called his parents but they're somewhere in the Bahamas."

I figured he was going to have a lot of zapping to do because there were a lot of people who would fit his criteria.

Later, we went to Robert's uncle's place in Falmouth. Could I sleep? No way. I must have guzzled six drinks and still I lay there in bed. My mind racing. Speeded out. Every hour I kept calling Rick's name, begging him to get me something to make me sleep. Apparently his tolerance was a lot better than mine after six weeks of getting stoned on meth, because he had no problem sleeping.

When I finally came to breakfast in the morning his uncle looked at me like I was crazy. Or maybe a fag or something.

When I flew home the next day I seemed to have rings under my eyes and felt like I had aged about three years in only three days. It took me about a week to get back to my old self, whatever that was.

My Fifth Year

When I got back to Steamboat in the fall of 1966, I found a lot of things had changed. There were actually three buildings on the hill some called Woodchuck overlooking the town. Enrollment was now up to about 120 students and they came from places as far away as South America, France and Norway.

The Norwegians could really ski and combined with a few local guys attending the college, YVC put together a ski team and even beat the University of Colorado ski team at some meet on the Eastern Slope.

There were five or six actually great teachers my second year at YVC. I had a private class twice weekly in philosophy and logic from Father Funk after the two other students dropped the class almost immediately. Although head of the Catholic Church in town, Funk was pretty much a chain smoker and he even enjoyed a glass of wine now and then. He worked on a PHD at the University of Illinois and I never saw him stumped by the most elaborate logic question imaginable.

The French teacher Mr. Reed was blind but could walk a half mile up to the campus with his dog, even in a blizzard. With an apparent photographic memory he memorized names and voices the first day and his hobby was restoring old cars. Of course Mr. Tolles class in international relations and world affairs was by far the most professional.

Three teachers opened a basement bar called Der Rathskeller which included a small restaurant so student and faculty relations were close-nit as long as students stayed away from the bar when stoned.

And that winter we had some of the deepest and driest champagne powder in the Rockies. With several new teachers being avid skiers, classes could be adjusted to accommodate the weather.

Meanwhile, Robert and I met a guy from Hayden who had just returned from four years in the marines and had been stationed in Japan where he was the only American in a karate class held outdoors even in the winter. Of course we convinced him to give us weekly classes for a nominal amount of money. This guy could jump in the air and land three kicks on a bag in an instant, each of which would have been rib breakers.

Like, Why Not Plant, Baby?

It's not like I can tell you anything
you haven't already thought a time or two:
It's not likely you'll find any cat
who has the big secret to pass on
which'll flip all those previous collections
of memory and perception.
So, like I'm not saying you should stop looking;
It's just that, like it's hard to find
what you're looking for
when you don't even know what you lost.
It's just like I thought you might want to pause here a bit,
I mean like, check out a few of my thoughts
before you sign back in.
It's like I just wanted to say slow the pace a bit,
maybe plant a few things before you move on.
I mean like you can never tell when you might
pass this way again.
And like, it might be nice to have something to
look back on: "Like that's my thing, and I did it."
And if it maybe gets wasted, you might, at least,
like know what you lost.
And anyway, like what you once picked up,
you won't have to find again.

Another Trip

One day in the winter there was great excitement around the school because someone had received a large stash of acid from back East. Amid the buzz, a number of students descended on the town and rented motel rooms or trailers to prepare for the big event.

I had dropped just that one time before and figured I had seen about all I needed to, but I was dating a girl I'll call Lucy who had never dropped so we couldn't think of any reason why we shouldn't. I mean I never knew anyone who had a bad trip and I wasn't even sure if there was such a thing. Sure, there were periods of a few minutes in which one thought ugly thoughts, but it always passed as soon as the mind tripped on something else.

Paul had a sort-of girlfriend and we went in on a trailer for the weekend. I remember having to convince him not to bring his guitar because he played some good riffs, but his specialty was not playing a song from start to finish. Besides, I had heard that people on acid have been known to trip out on bad conga drums for hours on end.

On the big night, the four of us broke what was supposed to be about 2,000 mics into eight pieces. I figured that 300 mics would be a solid trip and if it was good quality we wouldn't want to overdo it. After we had waited all of twenty minutes or so I said, "Well, we want to make sure we at least get off," so we downed the rest and all laid back on a double bed to wait for the rushes to hit our spine. It didn't take long.

One minute we were all lying on the bed watching the reflections of candles bouncing off the ceiling, the next minute we were all sitting up yelling, "Where are we?"

"It's...all...right. We're...just...taking a trip," I would say. Then we'd all laugh and lay back again. Then we'd be sitting up asking the same question. My whole body was rushing so hard I could hardly get the words out.

"Ok...no problem. Just...a...trip."

We lay next to each other on the bed, each in our separate

mental worlds, watching the colors, watching the spiral shaped, twisting inner core of mind and energy. Too high to even begin to think. Except: "Too hot...too many clothes on...take them off...be free...yes...totally free."

We shed our clothes, falling over each other, helping each other, struggling to free ourselves, to be unrestricted, to share, not to care. We threw everything in a heap.

We looked at each other, eyes all pupil. All black, yet so watery deep, and so beautiful.

"So beautiful...you're so beautiful...you too...women...look at them Paul...so beautiful...breasts...hair...lips...mouths...you too...and you...oh, touch...yes, touch."

Isn't there a heavier word than "groove?" We grooved each other. We – all of us – alive. The same moment. All that came before a frantic blur. 4,000 years in ten seconds. Then. Us. And now. Then we would pass on too. Just as quickly. The beauty of it all.

We began kissing. I, lost in her mouth. Her tongue. It told so much. Every sensation telling everything. Telling, giving, showing love.

"Paul," I said. "Bed...other room. Go make love...give... share."

They left. We were alone. We touched. My hand on her breast. No, in it. My hand was inside her breast! Oh, the beauty. She was touching me. I was excited. Was I? I reached down and touched myself. "No...I'm not," I laughed. "oh...I feel so..."

We were kissing and touching. I was laying back, flashes, colors, the twisting, spiraling ribbon-like energy, so 3 dimensional. No, 4 dimensional. I was seeing 4 dimensional in my mind. For the first time.

"Love," Lucy said. "Come in...me."

"Yes," I said.

Later. It was later. How much later? We hadn't made love. We forgot to make love. It couldn't have been more than a few minutes. But then we did make love.

More colors. Energy flashing everywhere. The wind blowing outside. Winter. Touching again. It was getting better and better.

"I love…I love…," Lucy said. "Oh…you're all there…in me so much."

And still we continued. There, more colors. More ribbons.

My god. Oh my god. We are fish. We are in a sea of ocean. We are in the ocean. No, we are birds…no I am a small…we are just worms. Inside each other. She in me, I in her…Oh, we are ameba… swimming in a fluid…no. Oh, god…we are cells, just cells…we are energy. Only energy.

And the rushing. We are rushing through space. Faster. We're moving faster. Stars. They're passing by. Planets. Asteroids… meteorites passing by…faster…we are light…passing it…even faster than light. The whole universe.

But what's that? Ahead…blue…a light…yellow and red and blue…brighter…closer…gates…I can see in the gates…and beyond…beautiful valleys and rivers…and birds…birds are there… I'm nearing the gates…I'm almost there…almost in…heaven? Is it…I can see…I…Oh God…God. I'm almost. Oh the sound…the music. Oh, the rushing sensation. We are one with all in the natural circle of the universe.

How can they kill? Let anyone starve? Gods. We are all gods. Alive for such a brief span on this planet. Then energy floating in space. Never destroyed. Scattered maybe. But never destroyed. Oh, the wondrous beauty. All an accident? You ask me to believe that? The beauty. Please. Please, I prayed. Let there be love everywhere. There has to be. Love cannot be an accident. It is too beautiful. Too total. What has become of Man?

****

It was later. We here holding each other, moaning, cooing. Everything still but so reflecting. Energy in everything moving. In the chair, the blanket...in Lucy's hair. Paul and She were back in the room. Dressing.

"No," I said. "Don't go out. Too dangerous. Someone might see."

"No. Out," She said. "We must go out." She was frantic. Was I imaging it? She was blowing it.

"Paul...go with her...don't let her out of your sight. Stay with her."

"Ok," he said. He looked up while putting on a sock. He was frantic. His eyes were so lit up. He was all eyes.

Then they were gone. And we were dressing and then we went out. It was snowing heavily. Flakes were coming down like giant cotton balls. Only even softer. So slowly and so soft. Sticking on everything, then bouncing off me or melting on me. It was two in the morning but there were groups of five or six people walking along the back streets, staying mostly in the alleys. Singing, dancing, laughing.

"Hello."

"I love you."

"I love you."

Students, I thought. All stoned. All walking around. What a giant bust. We went back to the trailer. Then we were making love again. And the thoughts kept coming. Oh, the wonderful beauty of it all. All of us alive. All of man that has come before. The total joy of it. How can people be so cruel to each other? How can they not help each other? Doesn't everyone want to love? To be loved?

On Climbing the Ladder

Like a little child she follows the
sweet sight and smell of lilac flowers
on the path that leads to the woods.
In the tall, mossy growth of greenery and thorn,
deeper she follows the inborn scent
in mysteriously cobwebbed natural archways.

Like that first smell of grass when everyone says,
"So that's it! I've smelled that before…
a long time ago."
And from somewhere in the back of the mind,
the hollow cell says, "Go, man, it's greenery calling."
And you dig it…you know it…always.
Who looks back when climbing the ladder
that takes you higher?
Like I mean one doesn't want to fall off,
right, man?
So up you go, and it's all for show.
You'll be back down again, though.
Not that you'll have missed anything:
Just the thoughts. Just the dull perception
of not knowing where you're going and,
most likely, where you've been.

****

How did I pass the time the rest of the semester? There wasn't
really much homework. I just continued to read and put out the school
paper. The townspeople seemed to love it; circulation was up to 500.
And I made love.

Then it was Christmas and I was home again with my parents,
but there was no way to explain where my mind was at. How can

you explain to a car salesman father that love is where it's at? That people all helping each other is the secret to a good life on this planet?

I skied quite a bit more after Christmas. Lucy was blowing my mind with so much talk of love. I was honest with her, though. I always told her there was no way I could marry for at least a few years. Not until I had figured out some way to beat the Army hassle. In her eyes I saw a different kind of love. It was a mother love. She wanted to mother me and I wasn't ready for that.

The Warp Theory of Light

I had an interesting conversation the other day with a fellow student whose father, I've heard, is one of the eight writers for Bob Hope. We both got a little stoned together and I can't remember if it was his father or a friend of his who actually had a first-hand experience with interspace travelers. It turns out he was informed that the universe is concave and if you didn't follow a beam of light, which is curved and always returns to its source, you could rather quickly go to another planet if you just knew which direction to go.

The way I try to explain it is that if you stood next to me and I walked with a ball of string about a mile or two, then around a telephone pole and back again, that would be the light of your star that I can actually see. But I could just take two steps and be on top of you if I knew where you really were. Oh, and there wouldn't be any passage of time when I'm in that black space between the two of us. It would be like you're on the other side of the rim of an upside down bowl.

First Narcs

The students have grown pretty close together. But it's not like last year when a bunch of us would go to the Hot Springs in the back of Strawberry Park and clothing was optional, but you really couldn't see anything because it was pretty dark with no lights or electricity. Sometimes a few of us stay there all night long and watch the sun rise.

But this year we had a great pig roast up near Hahn's Peak. Even a few people who aren't students showed up but the town is so small that everyone knows each other and it's not like anyone is going to get busted.

A lot of the merchants downtown probably know about students smoking grass based on what happened last week. Robert, Lucy and I were riding in his car about four miles out of town planning to get stoned. Robert noticed a blue sedan following us.

"Narcs on our tail," he said, matter-of-factly.

"You're sure," I said. "Could be tourists."

"Nope. Too early in the season."

He drove around a narrow bend in the road, then turned around quickly and brought the car to a stop in the narrowest part of the road. We sat there and waited. A half a minute later the blue sedan came around the corner. Two men were in it, wearing fishing clothes. They had to slow down almost to a complete stop to get by our car. We all looked at them smiling as they crept by, and they smiled back.

"Radio," Lucy said. "I swear. I saw a radio hanging from the dash."

"Yup," Robert said. "The plates are from Grand Junction. Narc headquarters. Come on. Let's get back into town."

We sped back into town, then split up, telling a few students what we saw. Up at the campus word got around quickly. At least 7 cars in the parking lot had their doors open and students were emptying ashtrays, sweeping out floor mats with whisk brooms, even one guy taking our his rear seat.

I just stood there laughing for about five minutes, checking out the serious expressions on everyone's face. Then I drove my car down to a gas station where I vacuumed it. I wasn't paranoid, but why take any chances?

Later some of the students drove downtown to get a closer look at the narcs. Someone saw them make a pass down Lincoln and six or seven students jumped into three cars and began following them. First from a distance, then they were practically tailgating them. I couldn't believe it!

The snake-like procession drove around a couple of back streets and then made another pass down Lincoln. Some other students were standing on the corner by Lyon drugstore eating ice cream. They all yelled and waved when the procession went by. A few even removed their sunglasses and held their eyes open wider with their fingers.

The narcs pulled up to the police station by the courthouse and hurried inside. The three student cars parked across the street with everyone wearing sunglasses. Finally the police chief came out and directed them to move along with his arm. Everyone laughed and sped away. The narcs never had a chance.

****

Robert and I drove to L.A. and then Palm Springs during spring break. But we spent one night in L.A. and went to a place called The Trip on Sunset Strip. It cost $5.00 cover to get in but the small club was packed with about 100 people.

The singer on stage was Donovan, and he was giving a great version of "Sunshine came softly through my window today..." when he fell off the stage in the middle of his set. I went into the men's room a couple of minutes later where I saw a guy yelling at Donovan and accusing him of being stoned on acid.

****

Spring skiing in late March and April in Steamboat is phenomenal. On any sunny day men wear shorts and girls are in halter tops. The Colorado sun at 9,500 feet gives a great red Indian suntan and the owl look is in when goggles or sunglasses are removed.

The days seemed to get longer and the full bloom of spring was suddenly upon us. The lush colors of the mountain valleys with their multi-shades of green are dotted with wildflowers popping up near the last remaining patches of snow. The rushing sounds of the streams and brooks, cold from upper mountain snow, give an uplifting background, almost soothing chant to the youthful dreams of eternal youth.

And yet we can't help talking in smaller circles about the upcoming summer and how many kids across the nation are into grass and rock fests and rock groups and long hair and marches and sit-downs. We talked of the war that drags on and of how many have died and were wounded and what we could do. Where was the country headed, we wondered, and what would come of the world?

Weren't students and young people throughout the world thinking about the same things we were? Would campuses be shut down until changes toward freedom of choice were made? Was someone in Vietnam dying for me? Could I face myself if I knew I had been forced to kill a human being? We needed a giant march for peace but how would this ever happen or even be allowed?

Finally one day I was standing with Lucy and a few other friends and they were helping me put on my cap and gown. Two students had been sent diplomas at midterm because of accumulated credits, but three of us were in the official first graduating ceremony. And a very hip college it was.

But, of course, I couldn't stop the same thoughts that kept repeating themselves: "Is this all there is? Is this all there is to it?"

Fall – 1967

I know it's only a matter of time before I'll be drafted into the Army. I thought about getting a draft deferment to go to graduate school, but find out I'm ineligible because it took me 5 years to get a BA degree.

I went to the head draft office in Chicago and took a test to see if I'm eligible for Army Intelligence School and maybe officer training school. Of course on the bottom of the test it said a lie-detector test will be administered at a later date and a felony charge could be possible for lying. So foolishly, I admit to trying pot a few times and dropping acid once. I'm called into a room an hour later and told I'm ineligible due to taking drugs and I have to fight to grab my paperwork out of some enlistment officer's hands for fear I'll be put on some CIA hit list. I figured they wrote me up anyway.

But now that I'm a wanted man, maybe I won't be drafted. There was no reason to go back to Steamboat, but Colorado was calling, so I figured I'd kill some time and head to Aspen to join the other college graduate ski bums.

It was only the first week of October and I landed a job as a bellboy at the Aspen Inn right at the base of Ajax Mountain near Little Nell. After doing maintenance by day for the hotel and getting drunk every night at the Hotel Jerome bar, the ski area opened and I realized I had one of the best jobs in the whole world.

I bunked in a basement room with a line cook and Whitey, another bellboy who was a crap dealer from Las Vegas for the past five years but who was taking a break from the fast lane. Whitey says he was making almost $100,000 a year, lived in a great pad, had his nails manicured weekly, but was drinking too much and cracked up two corvettes in three years. He needed a break.

I have a little blue jacket with gold buttons and a name tag. My job is to pick up guests at the airport, sometimes in a limo, and pack their bags to their rooms. The bags are incredibly heavy but I get tipped better by struggling. Plus there's a squirt can of kerosene

It is the Fall

by each fireplace and I get a bonus for setting 3 logs on fire in the fireplace the easy way.

If it's two or three guys and not couples or newlyweds, they always ask me the best places to eat and to hustle chicks. I always have a notepad and pen in my back pocket so pretty soon I've got a system down. I've already written down the best times to go to certain bars and restaurants so I pretend to scribble real fast, then rip out a page and whisper to them not to show my list to anyone else. Of course I mention that over-tipping will get them help from the bartenders. Oh, and it's ok to drop my name.

Pretty soon I'm getting a $20 tip per room and I'm making $150 to $200 a night if there's a lot of check ins. And when I go out I'm usually comp'ed drinks. Since I've got the swing shift, 3pm to around 11pm or so, at 2:30 pm I can ski right down to the Inn, jump a little wall, take my skis off at the pool and slip on my jacket and be set to go.

By the third week, I remember you can't buy liquor on Sundays in Colorado so I've got a mixed case of booze by my bunk and when a room needs booze I tell them I can sell them one of my personal bottles (that I crack open and take one sip out of beforehand) for a friendly, reasonable price.

One of the best things about the Aspen Inn is that there is a house band that plays every night. Two of the members, Lynn and Jenny were former Mouseketeers. The first song of the opening set every night is Sergeant Pepper's Lonely Hearts Club Band. The harmony is pitch perfect and it's a turn-away crowd every night.

One guy sits alone at a back table every night wearing a full fur hat. He barely acknowledges me. I ask around and hear his name is John Phillips and he's in the group Mammas and Papas. I notice he visits the band in their rooms each night and they all must have a hard time sleeping because their lights are usually on until almost dawn.

I hear that when a bartender wants to retire after five or more years he can sell his job for two to five thousand dollars. It seems like bullshit but I can figure in my head what they must be making in tips and it wouldn't take very long to make up the outlay.

I could have retired for the summer from this job, except the third week of January my parents sent me a letter which included my draft notice.

February 1968

I took a walk-through physical in some building in Chicago and three days later boarded a bus for Ft. Leonard Wood, Missouri.

Basic training is no harder than hell week at the fraternity when it comes to being yelled at or any kind of fear. I mean I know the drill sergeants aren't actually going to hit me. About 70 percent of the draftees in my company are Afro-Americans and most say they had a choice of jail or the Army from a judge. They're mostly 18 and I'm 22 so I keep to myself.

A couple of days ago the drill sergeant yelled "about face" and half the guys turned in the wrong direction. I got called out for breaking out laughing and had to low crawl holding my M-14 for about 100 yards by myself, then catch up for the 4am jog before breakfast. My belt buckle got so trashed I now keep two spare shiny ones in my locker.

****

"Pick up everything that don't grow. If you can't eat it or fuck it…piss on it."

"Listen. I been a sergeant in this man's army for eleven years now. You want to know where it's at in life? I'll tell you. Anytime you are in a position where people must go through you, or you are a source of their supply, you have power. And power is where it's at."

"I'll tell you, baby. I was religious, but I gave up religion as soon as I grew up. I was Catholic, you know, but there's the Pope sprinkling water with a million dollar ring on and two blocks away people are starving. I tell you we should burn them down. I go to church because it's peaceful."

****

Sign: "No war was ever won with compassion or conscious – kill"

****

It seemed to average about 10 degrees with a wind blowing at Fart Lost in the Woods, Missouri, but you can eat all you want in the 7 minutes allowed for each meal. I'm gaining weight and muscles like crazy. The "Daily Dozen" workout with pushups and sit-ups is a snap for me. It was no sweat shooting expert with the M-14, 7.62 rifle when you can rest it on something. We finally had about two days practice with the M-16 which is like a Mattel toy and I aced that, too. My best friend in basic ends up being a black guy from the south side of Chicago who had a clean record, a wife and young child and was drafted out of a good job at a steel mill. We both murmured softly during an afternoon lecture while two Vietnam vets were trying to get people to sign up for Airborne Ranger School after advanced infantry training.

"I know what they're going to do with most of us," he said. "Infantry. Got three friends before me in this shit and that's what they got."

When they passed around wish list sheets, I helped him write up three previous years' experience as the best and fastest prep and line cook at two chain restaurants. His goal in life is now to be a private chef and own his own restaurant. I'm pretty sure we both lost each other's phone numbers because we never crossed paths again.

In Limbo

It's now two weeks after basic training and everyone except me and two others has been shipped off to advanced infantry training. I'm an E-2 for doing a good job in basic, so I march the three of us off to three meals a day, sneaking ahead of the basic training companies by saying we're a special detachment. Sometimes I have us do a "change step at the halt" march in which we just jump straight up and replace our feet. It's good for a few laughs.

A sergeant just told me I'm assigned to the Ft. Leonard Wood newspaper as a reporter/photographer, I guess because I was editor of my college newspaper. The job is pretty easy. It's a 12,000 circulation paper, just covering whatever happens during basic training, and snapping photos of any unusual activities. If any celebrities arrive, I shoot photos of them with officers, making sure they get copies for their scrapbooks.

I work 8 to 5, six days a week with no roll calls. Every couple of nights we leave the post and drive past the string of pawn shops to the dive bars. I've already been promoted to E-3 because my job MOS requires it. Most of the girls you run into at the bars are engaged or promised to a soldier who is away somewhere on a one year tour of duty. A lot of them are in Germany, I hear, not in Vietnam.

I've been at this same routine now from May thru November and I'm pretty sure I'm safe. Until yesterday when I just got orders in the mail to report to Ft. Lewis, Washington on Dec. 18, 1968 for assignment to the Republic of Vietnam. That's it. I'm in the tunnel now and shooting out the other end. It's a little too late for the conscious objector scam. Goodbye Real World. Hello Dream World. Or is it the other way around?

A Quick Break

I have 10 days before I deploy and my parents are so depressed they let me fly down to Miami Beach for a six day vacation. I rented a Vespa motor scooter and drove up and down Collins Avenue. The bars stay open until 4am and one night I went to a place called the Wreck Bar. Members of various bands were up on the stage jamming. I think it was the Mothers of Invention and Jimmie Hendrix and the Soul Searchers. I knew I was lost in a moment.

I stood on a dock at dawn and just wanted to jump on a boat to Bimini. Then maybe hop on some freighter to South America. But I didn't want to let my parents down. And I wasn't going to be molested in some jail. Or face spending the rest of my life in Canada like some politician's son.

December 21, 1968

The 18-hour flight to Nam was straight from a high-fever nightmare. Everyone was chain-smoking cigarettes and I'd wake up for a half hour or so, turn on my air vent, then turn it off. They must have been conserving heat because my legs were wrapped in two blankets and still freezing.

There were six green berets sitting together in the front of the plane, all but one of them smoking cigars. They must have been on their second tour because half of them were staff sergeants in their mid-twenties. They kept making so much noise with their talking and laughing that someone asked a stewardess to tell them to hold it down, but one of them just slapped her on the ass.

Then some lieutenant got up and told them to "please hold it down just a little, fellas, huh?" They told him to shove it up his ass and if he didn't like it they'd see him when he got off the plane. Finally a six foot five 250-pound sergeant major got up, walked down the aisle and really put it to them.

"Now I'll tell you, and I'm only gonna tell you once you goddamn motherfuckers." He yelled. People were hanging out in the aisles to watch.

"This is my third trip to Nam and I'm gonna get some fucking sleep or I'm gonna take your fucking hats and cram 'em down your throat and I'm gonna do it right now if you don't shut up! You hear me?"

No one said a word and old Top stood over them and stared at them for a full 10 seconds. Then he turned around and started walking down the aisle while about 240 of us applauded and cheered, yelling, "right on." It was a very quiet flight after that.

The Next Day

I've arrived in Cam Rahn Bay, Vietnam. It's all sand
and I have no idea if I'm even supposed to step off the wooden
boardwalks. I don't even have any idea how to clean an M-16. I've
only even held one for a total of two days. Maybe advanced infantry
training would have helped.

For two hours they call out guys names for assignments in-
country and we listen to the moans or cheers as towns or U.S. bases
are called out: DaNang, Pleiku, Nha Trang, Phan Rang, Qui Nhon,
Dalat, Phu By... Finally I hear my name and last four numbers
followed by Cam Rahn Bay. I'm right here with a thousand or more
other guys on this giant beach of a base.

Headquarters Company is a series of hootches and wooden
buildings, each housing about 12 men. The lifers or higher up
enlisted men are in their own area. A lot of them are supply
sergeants and serving their second or even third tour. They do a lot
of trade outs and seem to barbeque steaks and burgers instead of
going to mess halls. Hell, they've even got hard booze instead of
beer and all seem to know each other like it's some big party. At
least roll calls or morning formations are rare.

I'm assigned to the information office in the headquarters
building. There are two other guys with the same MOS as I and
I'm promoted to Specialist E-4 right away. One guy has a great,
slow speaking western drawl and hails from Deadwood, S.D. The
other is a college graduate from St. Bonaventure who only wants to
talk basketball. He doesn't think much of Bradley's prowess in the
Missouri valley NIT playoffs.

My captain in charge is a reservist stock broker from New York
who plainly has no intention of leaving the sanctuary of Cam Rahn
unless he can get a direct flight to Saigon to party at the officers'
club, possibly with real world reporters.

I'm issued 2 Leica cameras and a bulky reel to reel tape
recorder. My first job is to take photos with a brief caption of fellow

soldiers to be sent out for their home town newspapers. I'm also to record 30 or 60 second spots on tape for hometown radio stations. My territory apparently is everything north of Saigon up to the DMZ.

Whenever I go off base I usually draw out a 45 handgun, or sometimes also an M-I carbine with a banana clip which is so old I don't even have to check it back in. I enjoy traveling with a vet treating hoof and mouth disease and deliveries of supplies, often sent by charities back home to orphanages as far out as Ban Me Thuot.

I'm finally going out in the field by usually by chopper to small base camps. Half the guys don't even want their photos taken, but their officers demand it or threaten to cancel a chance for a one week R & R out of country.

At a small camp about 20 miles from Ban Me Thuot I catch a photo of a projectile half way out of a 175 at 1,000th of a second. I later find out it makes the front page in a bunch of newspapers back in the states. Any good shots I take are laid out on a table in Saigon for the wire services to pick up. There are no photo credits, though.

That 175 can go something like 20 miles or more, accurate to one-half a football field. When it comes out of the barrel it seems to drop down a little then whoosh it takes off in the air like a bat out of hell. The little base camps are zeroed in on the fence lines of the bigger bases so they can scare off any Charlies with satchel charges. But the poor guys at the little bases live under sandbags and sometimes take incoming just about every night. I do my best to avoid spending the night at any little outposts.

I know that if you're on a convoy and you start taking sniper fire, everyone just leans out and empties magazines as fast as he can to gain firepower. No one is going to stop and see if they actually hit anyone or not. And when you get scared your mouth's so dry you can't even drink out of a canteen.

Another guy in my office and I got a 2-day in-country pass to drive a jeep up to Nha Trang to check out the press club there. We've got patches sewn on our sleeves that say "Official U.S. Army Correspondent" and no one hassles us for passes anymore. It's about an hour drive up the coast on a hot, humid day and we lower the windshield to grab the wind and sights and smell of fresh cut grass and charcoal smoke from mud and stone kilns. We had just cracked a couple of beers and were enjoying the greenery when we hear two whisses and realize bullets had actually zipped by us. Some damn gook in a field was taking pot shots at our jeep. We barreled up to 60 and soon came roaring into a totally picturesque town on the ocean like something out of a movie set.

Girls riding on the back of motorbikes were holding parasols and smiling to each other. Sometimes whole families were packed onto a motorbike with groceries in a basket in front. The backdrop was a turquoise blue ocean to the east with sandy beaches up to the road. A resort brochure had popped up in the middle of what was supposed to be a war zone.

We located the international press club, a three story building with a little courtyard and a four stool bar. There was no sign of anyone from any press organization. An old man with a broom understood French better than English, which seemed natural since this was formally French Indonesia.

After numerous beers my buddy and I took a walk around 10 pm but after only three blocks we suddenly found ourselves surrounded by five kids on motorbikes who started circling around us, taunting us in Vietnamese.

"They're cowboys," my friend yelled. We both pulled out our 45s and fired a few shots in the air to scare them off. Then we quick-timed it back to the club before Army MPs could zero in on our location. A couple of hits of pot and we called it a night.

One of the scariest parts of my whole Vietnam experience had to be the day I was up in a chopper, laying on my stomach trying to get some good aerial photos. The chopper suddenly banked down and left sideways and I slid right out the door almost past my waist. Luckily the door gunner was just going to warn me about not being strapped in and grabbed my shirt with both hands. He and another guy dragged me in.

The pilot who looked to be about 18 glanced back laughing. I tried to hide the fact that my hands were shaking and I felt like throwing up. From then on I made up any excuse I could think of to avoid getting back on a chopper. The slight fear I had of heights was now solidified.

Hong Kong

Finally I was up for a one week R & R and decided to travel with a planeload of other G.I.s in awkward street clothes to Hong Kong. I went through the famous customs with everyone else on the plane and was glad I didn't try to bring anything into the country. One guy, they would tear apart his camera. The next, they would look him dead in the eye while unrolling his toothpaste tube. With me, I was stared down while they probed my small can of talcum powder with a thin wire.

I found out later, Hong Kong has plenty of opium and hash, but officials just didn't want to see any more of the famous GI pot, laced with all the good stuff from the Triangle. I remembered one afternoon in Cam Rahn when I was sitting in a portable john with a joint and heard footsteps on the wooden boardwalk. I peeked out and it was a lifer coming my way. I looked down, still had a half of a joint in my hand but couldn't remember how long I had been sitting there, or even where I was, for that matter. I must have dozed off.

I had a small guide book about Hong Kong and spent my days wandering about the city enjoying the three S's: sights, sounds and smells. The city seemed amazingly safe in the evening. Every bar I wondered into had a dozen or more beautiful, painted call girls, each of whom had special cards which they could leave at the front desk if you wanted to take them back to a hotel room. I was paranoid of diseases and got so drunk every day that I wasn't really tempted.

I ordered, was fitted the next day and picked up a couple of suits and got a $500 Nikon camera for $250. Then one night I sauntered into a practically empty bar where I sat next to two older, obviously drunk Australian men. They immediately recognized me as a Vietnam soldier on my R & R and started trying to pick a fight with me. Just as I was starting to get off my barstool to defend myself, a short but very stocky bouncer walked up to them and said, "No. First you pay your tab. Then you can fight."

"Well, fuck you, mate," the taller one said. "We've been here all day and we'll damn well pay our tab when we're good and ready."

Almost instantly the bouncer grabbed him by the lapels again and smacked him in the center of his forehead with the top of his own head. The Aussie went down to his knees, but slowly got back to his feet again and said, "Now we're not going to pay our tab at all."

He already had a bump on his forehead the size of an egg. But the short Chinese bouncer grabbed him by the lapels again and smacked him again with his head in the exact same spot. Blood splattered in the air. I quietly thanked the bartender as I eased my way toward the front door.

The last night I finally decided to ask a beautiful young girl at the bar if she wished to come up and see my room. Of course I also had the bright idea to ask her if she could possibly also get a small bud of hash to put us in the mood. It was about 6 pm when we got to my room. I took three pretty strong hits of the hash with a crudely improvised pipe I made and suggested we go out to dinner first.

Apparently I made it as far as the lobby before she and the bellboy helped me back up to my room because the next thing I remembered was being in bed with a wet washcloth on my head and the phone ringing. It was the same girl confirming my suspicions: yes, she said, it was opium as there was no hash around. She said she gave the bellboy 20 bucks of my money to keep his eyes closed and she also borrowed my watch for payment as I must have hidden any other money I might have had. She just wanted to make sure I wasn't going to turn her in or the police might get involved and we'd all be in trouble.

It was one of those cheap $15 watches anyway, and I was sure looking forward to getting back to the safety of Vietnam.

****

James   77

I had it pretty easy. I really did. I mostly just travel around taking pictures, writing stories for Army publications and home town news releases, little featurettes on sweeps, convoys and the rest. And yet something…something kept rising up in me. Something about the absurdity, the money being spent, the lives.

Yes, I think it was the lives lost. The men, who were really changed, spent out at 20, sick, diseased, disillusioned, wounded, stoned, bent-shaped and twisted. The crooked sergeants, the chickens and the gung-ho: all the same. There was something about the lack of conviction in the cause that everyone felt, and yet the lives lost. The young wag that threw up blood in front of me and said, I think I've got an ulcer but they won't let me go to the hospital."

It was like a spirit was flooding over me. Every time a shell went out, energy kept clawing at my mind. I was to live and he was to die. The peasants by the side of the road, squatting to relieve themselves while someone laughed and threw a can of rations at them as we drove by.

And then there were the news teams with their human-interest 6 o'clock reports, two minutes allowed, then up and away. Coverage to wet appetites in the cocktail hour body counts that made us look like we were winning the war or conflict or whatever it is.

It was such a game – such a real game – that we all seemed to be acting out our parts. All bit-players with no real lead. I never understood the plot.

Last Call

I've got less than one month left in-country. It's becoming increasingly clear that the war stories guys in the rear are telling are usually something they heard from the guys who are mostly out in the field every day. And most of the guys who see real action on a daily basis don't talk about what they've seen or done. So no one who talks about anything can be trusted.

I heard a story about a guy who had a similar job to mine and he said one time he was up in a chopper when they were called down to pick up a couple of Intel guys who had two VC prisoners. This guy said as soon as they got a few hundred feet up in the air, the Intel guy just shoved one of the VC out the door of the chopper.

My friend asked him why he did that, "'cause it was just murder." He said because it would make the other guy give up information a lot easier than just threatening him. My friend said he told him it just wasn't right. Then he was promptly told that his whole 201 files were in Saigon or Long Bihn and if he said a word about what happened, he'd find out where his parents lived back home and his buddies there knew what to do.

I'm just glad that something like that never happened to me.

I had less than 5 months left in my two year draft tour of duty so I was going to be discharged as soon as I got back to the States. The Army didn't want a bunch of guys with just a few months left to start telling stories around a bunch of guys in basic training who might think about going AWOL.

Home December 21, 1969

I arrived at Ft. Lewis, Washington after an 18 hour flight on no sleep, then spent about 20 hours getting processed out, was gifted a lined, olive drab trench coat and made it onto an airplane heading to Chicago in uniform. I hit it off with a stewardess and she bumped me up to first class and gave me a bottle of champagne. But that was the last kindness toward me I ever felt again in uniform.

I remember walking through O'Hara airport toward the baggage claim and people staring at me with my obvious Vietnam suntan like I had done something wrong rather than serving my country. The cab driver went out of his way not to ask me any questions.

I surprised my parents at 2 a.m. with a knock at the door because they weren't expecting me until a few days later on Christmas Eve. We stayed up until 4 in the morning talking and I'm sure they could tell I was pretty tired and pretty drunk as well.

My dad had saved all the letters and photos I had sent home. My mother said they watched the nightly news every evening during dinner. My dad, apparently, had an extra martini or two whenever they flashed the daily body count of us against the enemy.

For the first several weeks I settled into a schedule of up at noon, driving around during the day and then off to the bars after dinner, either locally or in Chicago. Finally I was confronted at 2:30 a.m. and my dad said it was either look for a job or move out of the house. Most of the other guys I knew took two to four months off after Vietnam unless they had some good job to go back to.

U.P.I.

I had met a couple of guys in Nam who worked for the wire service United Press International and had even given them a few tips on possible stories, so I slipped on one of my Hong Kong suits and walked into the UPI office halfway up the Tribune building on Michigan Avenue.

During a one hour, walk-in interview I flashed some pictures and copies of stories I had written which had made stateside newspapers and Stars and Stripes and was promptly offered a one month trial job on the swing shift.

I scored a tiny apartment on the top floor of a three story building hidden between high rises one block off Michigan Avenue. I was only six blocks from Old Town and three blocks from plenty of singles bars.

The UPI office in Chicago was in a large room with about 20 mostly manual typewriters banging away, highlighted by the ringing of bells, teletype machines and phones ringing. As the Midwest bureau, 7 states fed stories into us which we sent out nationally if they warranted attention.

Everything was typed onto "books" consisting of four pages. After an editor's check, one copy went to news release on the wires, one to radio copy for rewrite to rip and read stations, and another to TTS or justified type for papers to receive in column inch size to paste up and shoot to print. There were usually four union guys whose only job was to retype what reporters had written and send it over the wires.

Importance of stories coming in or going out was by bells ringing. When bells sounded, it was a news flash with a breaking news bulletin to follow. Anyone not super busy would dash over to the teletype to see what earth-shaking story could justify bells.

The first month I was on swing shift, 3 p.m. to midnight. I typed up six "books" with blank spaces ready for my phone calls from the Chicago Board of Trade. With my headset on I waited for the call from our man on the floor and then typed in the daily closings, from corn to pork bellies, never fully understanding what that might mean. I had never made so many fractions on a typewriter in my life.

Luckily I soon got promoted to the rewrite horseshoe desk because a guy who had only been there two months wasn't cutting it at rewrite. The poor guy got my job.

There's Dirt in the Slums

Funny, how when I walk through slums
I feel guilty.
No matter what I'm wearing, my clothes
seem a little too nice: I feel obvious,
out of place, just a little guilty.
I don't feel wanted.

But in the suburbs, the really rich ones,
my clothes and I feel proud.
Though I may look out of place,
I feel physically proud.
And I never feel guilty.
I feel as though I belong and I'm needed.

We always complain about garbage in the alley,
but that's what alleys were made for.
They're made for garbage.
It's just a hunch, but I figure people walk
pretty tall in heaven.
I'm pretty sure they crawl in hell.

****

It was lucky I came into work early today because just as
everyone guessed the jury was going to reach a decision on the
Chicago 7 trial. There were two extra old-timers at the big desk
and sure enough, we got a call from our man covering the trial.
Everyone was wearing headsets to listen in to the phone call, but the
rewrite men started yelling back and forth to each other.
"I've got Davis in the fourth. You take Kunstler in the sixth."
The guys were so pro they were taking turns writing paragraphs, all
putting one story together, adding background information about

charges, but ready to have a complete story ready to hit the wires without rewrite.

An hour or so later we learned we had beat the AP wire service by over 30 minutes so every paper and radio station was going with UPI across the country. Bells were still ringing when the last paragraph went out and the whole room was cheering.

I checked out a newspaper ad today and bought a 1969 Matchless 750cc motorcycle with high bars for only $1,200. It leaks a little oil, but can do a wheelie, even popping into third gear. One street level below Michigan Avenue is a great joint called the Billy Goat and instead of walking or catching a bus to work I chain my bike to a girder by the front door during my shift.

The Billy Goat specializes in hamburgers and cheeseburgers, but drinking is what it's really all about. The clientele is mostly cops, firemen and reporters. The place is open 24 hours a day and some guys are getting off work and drinking hard while others are slamming down coffee and rolls and sobering up to go to work. My bike is safe and I've got a UPI press card with photo, endorsed by the Chicago Police Dept. on the back.

I got off work as usual at midnight today, and was listening to the beautiful sound of my bike's exhaust echoing off the buildings in downtown Chicago when I got pulled over by a couple of cops by the Marshall Field store. They just wanted to know what kind of bike I had. They said Norton in England bought out Matchless, but I had a sweet sounding machine. And, oh, by the way, my handle bars were not technically legal.

I always park my bike behind my 3 story building when I go out because I've already let it go down a couple of times at stop signs. And this was when I was sober. Luckily the bike only weighs about 420 pounds and I can lift it upright again using a lot of leg strength.

The swing shift, getting off at midnight, is great because most of the bars don't even close until 4 a.m. Tonight I went to a place with a waiting line, but no cover and got in easily using my press card. A band called Chicago was playing and they sounded great with all the horns and great harmony. About 2 a.m. Hugh Hefner walked in with an entourage of six girls who all could have been playmates. I guess his mansion is only about four blocks north of the place.

I got sent out today to cover a speech being given by Lyndon Johnson and got some points by calling in some good quotes when he was only about a third of the way through his speech so we got a fast lead on the other wire services. When I got to the location I noticed there were only six phone booths so I used the old trick of unscrewing the receiver's speaker and putting an out of order sign on the phone. There's nothing worse than seeing any kind of breaking story and not being able to find a phone.

Today I ran into a girl I had met in Chicago in the two week break before I went to Nam. She said she had moved and has a steady boyfriend now. I forgot that I had sent her some pot from Nam. I had bought one of those cheap wooden vases, then wrapped the pot about three times in clear wrap, then poured wax over it and set a wick in it. She said just two hits got everyone stoned and it was actually too good to get high on and go out in public.

It's the last week of August, 1970 and I'm getting bored with what is mostly a rewrite job at UPI. I've submitted a request to be assigned to Vietnam so I can actually get outside and be a reporter.

It's been two weeks and my request is denied. There is a long waiting list of UPI reporters across the country who want to leave their desk jobs. I've given my two-week notice.

****

Ode to Carl Sandburg

What spaced-out time in streets of grime,
dear old city hassles: it's not all put-down.
I miss your lights, your color

and your many painted faces.
I could spend a summer night or two, walking
in your busy night life clip-joint sections,
just to have a look.
I could smell in spring or fall, and perhaps,
stop on a dark winter day to have a drink
or a cup of coffee when I think I really need it.

But for the rest, save a friend or two,
I could do without you, live and breathe
apart from you – you no longer hold the charm
of youth's false security arm.
And mostly, I don't need your peoples,
want your death or charming steeples,
I prefer the out-of-doors.

So goodbye follies, new york, chicago,
miami and old cold boston.
See ya frisco, seattle, denver,
dallas, kansas city and l.a.
Read about you in the papers,
see your pictures in newsweeklies.
I know you'll make and shake it on your own.

Just please be gentle if I should pass through;
hold your fears to minor growls.
I'll respect you for your bigness,
but that, I know, is where it ends.

Colorado Calling...Again

It's September 15th and I've arranged to have my Matchless 750 included in a truck shipment going to Denver, Colorado. My father is not understanding my decision, but concedes I have to do what is best for me. I think he believes I am shell-shocked or something. I make a mental note not to bring up the subject of having been to Vietnam with anyone from now on.

I flew into Denver and took a cab to a truck depot a few miles from the airport. I roped a duffle bag on the back, slipped on a 30lb backpack and at noon I'm heading out of Denver destined for Steamboat Springs.

It must have been the 70s in Denver but I'm forced to stop on Berthoud Pass where I hurriedly start putting on 2 sweaters, another pair of pants and even mittens because my hands are freezing and I don't have any gloves.

The fall colors are spectacular, just like I've been dreaming about. And the smells change around every corner on a motorcycle with no wind protection: aspen, spruce, Douglas fir, ponderosa pine...I stop again and wrap a scarf over my nose and mouth. Jesus, it must be below 30 degrees at 70 mph. Particularly in the long stretches of shade.

Finally I stop at the top of Rabbit Ears Pass on Highway 40 and look to the right where the rock formation actually does resemble rabbit ears. It's warming up but I don't shed any clothes until I hit main street. It feels like 65 degrees at 4 p.m. and it's nearly October. But that's how I'll always remember Colorado. The sun is almost always out if it's not an afternoon summer shower or a winter's snowstorm. But if you stand in the sun a sweater is enough if you're out of the wind. And the air can't be any fresher when you're at 7,000 feet. God I feel at home in Colorado.

Robert is married and living in a small cabin next to The Barn in the middle of Strawberry Park. I spent the fall fishing by the three lakes on the top of Buffalo Pass and up in Little and Big Red parks near Hahn's Peak. Robert and I don't see another soul when we're camping but know that some day thousands of people will probably discover the Routt County forests.

I have decided to sell the bike but not just because winter is coming. I dumped it three times in one day trying to show off doing wheelies. I drink too much to have only two wheels under me. And even with thinner oil, I can't seem to kick start it when it's below freezing. It will only start if it is parked on top of a hill.

I've been working as a desk clerk at the Harbor Hotel. The town is still so small that if a red light blinks on a wire hanging across the street from the Harbor, the one cop on duty is supposed to call a number to see who needs him. It's the duty of the cop to meet the 3 a.m. bus which stops at the hotel, check for strangers and give locals a ride home.

Funny how the town got a nautical theme just because some trappers thought they heard a steamboat and were at the mouth of the Yampa River, only to find some bubbling sulfur and hot springs making a bunch of noise. Of course, people had to keep throwing rocks and stuff into the springs until all the sounds were gone.

Business is booming at the base of the ski area. The Inn at Thunderhead is located at the base of the ski area and shops and several bars are clumped together in a section known as Ski Time Square. Robert and I acquire jobs at a small bar called the Button Bush, owned by a trio who began their day with Tom Collins at 11 a.m.

We were present the day Skeeter Werner, sister of famed skier Buddy Werner, actually was duped into falling for the old bar game called the funnel trick. While she rocked her head back and balanced a quarter on her forehead, she was challenged to drop the coin into a funnel placed down the front of her ski pants. Naturally, nearly one half of a pitcher of beer was poured down the funnel before she caught on to what was happening. I was surprised to find that she had a great sense of humor and took the whole thing quite well as a dozen patrons whooped and hollered in joy. She wasn't at all as

It is the Fall

straight-laced as so many people thought.

I've landed a job at the weekly Steamboat Pilot newspaper as a reporter. The paper was started by Chuck Leckenby's grandfather, but he's primarily interested in the business end of the paper which is printing and office supplies. There's also good money in printing legal notices if you're the official county paper.

Land is starting to sell like crazy and a Dallas firm called LTV has bought the ski area. I'm now consumed by evening meetings that drag on forever: the town board, county commissioners, city and county planning commissions, etc.

The town board previously just submitted minutes of their meetings to the paper. Now I'm attending and putting quotes in stories. The mayor promises to give Leckenby "complete minutes" of meetings if he will just stop sending me and stop my quotes of what people say before the story can be approved.

The only other reporter is Dee Richards, a divorced mother of four grown children, and a few stringers from small towns like Maybell and Hahn's Peak. We try to stress the need for locals to elect intelligent board members. But no one is going to stop the bankers and realtors. Steamboat is on the map.

There are about 80 ski bums and hippies living in town now. Some of the best skiers, I've heard, have left town in the two years I was gone and headed to an upcoming place called Telluride. The snow is said to be even deeper and the ski runs steeper.

In the fall of 1971 I get a call to go to the courthouse where they're bringing in a bunch of hippies caught in a drug sweep. As they bring in people in cuffs I realize I know just about everyone. The cops and town leaders have hired a couple of professional bounty narcs with beards who have been smoking pot and buying pot for months with locals in town.

It isn't long before the standard rule of thumb in town is "if he hasn't lived here for at least a year or doesn't own property, you don't do any drug deals with him and don't bring him to my house."

June 1972

I have decided to take a leave of absence from the paper and travel to Europe for the summer. It's something that I promised myself I would do when I was in Vietnam, and it seems like all I've ever done is work.

I found that by showing my student ID from YVC I'm able to get a first class Euro rail pass for only $300. I first arrived in New York City the last week of June and looked up my old buddy Doug who lives on East 79th between 1st and York. His father is still president of some big bank and Doug took me to the New York Athletic Club.

I can honestly say this was the first and last time I ever wore only a towel and sat around an indoor swimming pool eating a steak sandwich while watching a clothing optional array of red-faced tycoons swimming. Some of the fat old gray-haired farts were totally naked playing gin and drinking martinis. They all looked like cartoon characters in the New Yorker. They didn't have their gold chain necklaces and diamond pinkies in their lockers either.

We went back to the NYAC for dinner, too. I remember a cocky wine steward with a silver cup hanging on a chain around his neck taking Doug's order for a 1959 Mouton Rothschild cabernet sauvignon. It was like $100 for the bottle and we had to let it breathe for an hour.

When we finally had our first sip Doug called over the wine Stewart and demanded he taste and review it.

"It's very good, sir," he reported, adding, "but I believe it's no better than the 1965 Laffite that I recommended." And off he scampered. Shit, what an asshole.

The next night Doug took me to Elaine's which was a short walk from his apartment. Apparently he went there a few times before because Elaine herself actually acknowledged him. I figured it was more likely he was known as a big tipper. The next morning I flew off to Europe.

I arrived in Amsterdam and had a cab drop me off at the downtown train station with an absurdly large, overweight yellow backpack, plus sleeping bag and a smaller North face yellow shoulder pack with a combined weight of over 50 pounds. I was going to get in great shape.

Within 30 minutes at a bar across from the station I met two local couples who put me up for free for two days after introducing me to the local custom of downing shots of gin between beers.

The second night they took me to a folk bar where the solo guitarist on stage was replacing a broken metal string.

"You do that all the time," I yelled out, receiving a chorus of "boo...shut up" from the crowd. But the guitarist was Chuck Pyle from YVC whom I had recognized. Luckily he called me up on stage and introduced me before I could be thrown out.

I took the train up through Denmark and Norway where my goal was to look up my father's unseen relatives. The beauty of the first class train pass was that as soon as I rolled out my sleeping bag across three seats, people would look in, but no one wanted to join me in my compartment.

Without much trouble I located Jens from college who was working with his father in downtown Oslo. A government office using only my grandfather's name was able to locate relatives within 30 minutes. I also learned that if you don't have blood relatives in Norway, forget any idea of immigrating to that country.

After a two hour reunion with Jens providing translation, I spent two nights at his parent's cabin in Bergen. I liked the fact that no houses can be built within close proximity to any mountain ridge or peak. If I had been ready to settle down I would have asked Jen's sister to marry me in a heartbeat.

****

The Secret

In the bars of Paris
in 1972 Dietrich
knew the secret of life.

"Who is Dietrich?" he said.
"Where is Dietrich? There
is no Dietrich.
He doesn't exist."

"What you have to know,"
he continued, "that's the
secret: there is no secret!
You have to know that; that
is the secret to life."

"But," he concluded, "We all
know that. We've just forgotten.
But, how could we have forgotten
the secret to life?"

In the bars of Paris
and in others around the world,
people continue questioning,
searching, seeking
for the secret to life.

✳✳✳✳✳✳✳✳✳✳✳✳✳✳✳✳✳✳✳✳✳✳✳✳✳✳✳✳

I traveled by train down through Germany, saw a buxom
woman kick two drunk tourists out of the Haufbrauhouse, and on to
Rome where I saw the wealth in the Vatican museum while outside
broke beggars sat waiting for tourist's tips.

Whatever city I visited if I didn't want to pay for a room, I just left a bar at 10 p.m., hopped on a train and slept in a "private" compartment and five hours later took another train back into the city for another day of wandering.

Finally I arrived at Torremolinos on the southern tip of Spain. It was a gathering place for young, backpacking tourists, many from Europe. Rooms were cheap and wine could be had for as little as a few cents a glass. Twice a day I ate paella which is yellow rice and any number of fish and seafood items mixed in. It is only 65 cents at a local fishermen's bar. The big gathering place is Notra Dias or night and day. The bar never closes. I find myself with a crowd who drinks till dawn, then sleeps on the beach during the day. Three weeks seem to have flown by and I head toward Amsterdam with only two days remaining on my rail pass. But not before I took the ferry over and back and spent one night in Tangiers, Morocco where I got lost wandering in the casaba section and had to pay a kid to get me back to the ferry.

Drifting 1972

Ah, sweet Torremolinos, Spain,
come to me, baby, overnight
legendary resortville of Michner's
recent coup setting: but where
are "The Drifters?"
They're there, man,
but so wasted drunk they can
barely stand up at night,
dragging themselves from
British or German-owned bars
and pubs, singing sweet hellos
and rapping yesterday's history
of drunks and sexual conquests,
not to mention the occasional
Moroccan hash bust, toilet-flushing
near misses or even suicides:
"We had a self-inflicted stabbing
in my hotel last week. Luckily he
held his gut, walked out the door
and bled to death in the street.
The police won't close the hotel,
but we'll have to cool it for a while."

Fall 1972

I'm back in Steamboat Springs and working at the Pilot again, also continuing to put out the free weekly tourist guide, the Steamboat Whistle (how nautical it all is). And I'm living in reporter Richards' basement, as she takes in boarders for free and I'm the fourth. She's still up at 5 a.m., at work by 7 and writes copy in the evenings at home.

Dinner is served every night except Sunday at 6 p.m. The other guys are locals who've moved out of home and are ski patrolmen in the winter and work construction in the summer with plans of eventually going to college. She refuses rent or payment for her hospitality. One of the guys brings home a puppy, half boxer and half Heinz-57, found at the ski area and named "George."

It's mostly lengthy planning commission meetings and endless discussions about plats for proposed subdivisions and the incredible struggle to finally adopt city and county zoning regulations.

I did have some fun when the railroad donated the old train depot to the city because their only use for the tracks now would be coal shipments. Why would they run a passenger train on one of the most beautiful stretches in the country if they couldn't make any money from it? I wrote a lengthy sidebar about the worn and dusty boards and benches where so many boys said their farewells before going off to the wars while waiting for a train. A retired realtor living on top of what is called goat hill above town behind the hospital read the article and donated money so the depot can become an arts center for the town.

I find myself writing last minute copy at the Old Town Pub (formerly The Cameo) next to the courthouse the night before copy is due. I gain the uncomfortable handle "Scoop," said with digging sarcasm.

Tuesday and Wednesday at the Pilot newspaper are the layout days where we wax justified type copy and "paste" it up on the page layouts. With the offset printer purchased while I was in the Army, it's a far cry from the hot lead style press when I was putting out the college paper The Talisman.

The only problem with writing for a weekly paper is the tendency to write too creatively, perfecting the piece for all to read, frequently adding sidebar stories. It's a far cry from the rewrite desk at UPI where I could knock out the national weather survey in 30 minutes, consolidating weather highlights wired in from across the country.

I've located a small cabin behind town on more than 600 acres adjoining the Stevens College/Perry Mansfield summer camp. The land is actually owned by a rancher who sold the property but can remain in his ranch house as caretaker for the rest of his life. My access is up a road behind town.

George is my dog now and wears a red dog pack and gives out free copies of The Whistle tourist guide as we walk around the ski area. He has been issued a ski pass with photo and pass number K-9.

The great thing about this cabin is that two-thirds up the driveway, I can look back over the entire town and Howelsen Hill. Then I drop down into a little valley and can just see part of Strawberry Park and the ski area.

Almost year-round the smell of sage permeates the fields and my cabin. In the winter it's snowshoes if I'm carrying a heavy pack or cross country skis if I'm light. The total distance up the road, across the meadow and down to my two-room "home" is about a half mile. George and I are in heaven.

I met a guy at a bar who said he owns a jack burro he saved from some hunters who made him run 5 miles tied to the back of a pickup truck. I pay him $50 and rent a small U-Haul and drive all the way to Fairplay, Colorado. The town used to make national news in the winter as the coldest spot in the U.S. on some days. It's almost a ghost town now, but the beauty of the mountains that high is stunning.

He's a big, white burro and after much prodding, I load him into the trailer and drive him back to my place behind town which, luckily, is fenced around my rental cabin.

The seasons are going by, land prices are climbing and applications for subdivisions and condominiums at the base of the ski area and any hill facing it are soaring.

The Middle Seventies

I hear that an investment group which purchased 640 acres in the back of Strawberry Park is forced to pull out because the owner has passed away, leaving the parcel to his son who does not want to sell. But 40 acres have already been cleared to sell for $1,000 an acre.

It's a beautiful parcel, a box canyon with a year-round brook running through it. The north and east side have a steep slope with hundreds of pine trees, leaving only 5 or 6 acres of meadow; the remainder is thick with aspen. From on top of a hill I can overlook Strawberry Park and get a glimpse of a prep school across the road.

In a matter of days I've pushed an offer through and a friend at the bank who is also a Vietnam Vet helped me secure a loan.

A ditch circles the property, later crossing above the Park and meandering for miles until it irrigates farmland along the Elk River Road. The moment I walked the land in late spring and viewed the wild flowers, I knew the land was meant for me.

It turns out that two of the acres actually fall on property the prep school has always used as a soccer field. The headmaster convinces me to sell the land to the school with his word that the land will not be used as a building site. I agree and now have enough money to build a cabin.

And about this time, the paper was growing and two new reporters were hired. One is a recent college graduate, originally from California, and as I showed her around the newspaper I lost my heart to her. I've been waiting my whole life to finally fall in love.

The Cabin

No matter how well you plan it, even knowing how hard
the winter is going to be at 7,000 feet, houses never seem to start
construction in Routt County until the fall. It's the first week of
September and I've assembled Robert, now my next door neighbor,
and three other more experienced carpenters.

Normally at this elevation it would be smartest to build on
land in the spot where snow melts first in the spring – the hot spot.
But I've saved that spot for a garden and a future location for a
Big House when I make it big. I've chosen a site among the pines,
across the steam.

We build a sturdy bridge first, tying it in to some boulders
by driving spikes into cracks. For wood, we've chosen a small
mill in Yampa about 20 miles from Steamboat. It's run by three
Scandinavian brothers who harvest primarily standing dead lodge
pole pine trees, mostly killed by beetles in a major infestation about
30 years ago.

The mill's major buyers use the timber in underground mines
for shearing. The pine has wind splits, but on end withstands
tremendous weight. And, I hear, the wood will groan and sing,
giving warning if it's under too much stress, unlike green wood.

The mill primarily does rough cut, and we plan and order 6 x
8s and 2 x 10s. Studs are true 2 x 4s. Our plan is a post and beam
structure with capitals on top of the posts. I hire a backhoe to dig 12
holes, each four feet deep, well below the frost line. After pouring
cement pads we brace cardboard sono tubes and fill them with
cement and rebar. The 18 by 22 foot rectangle is secured together by
bottom plates.

The front of the cabin will be six feet above ground to allow for
the depth of snow in the winter. I don't want to shovel my way out
the front door in the mornings. All power is by a Honda generator
and two carpenters can't use a worm drive saw at the same time.

It's late October and we no longer have to sweep snow off the deck because we are finally roofing with 2 x 10s and a Christmas tree is nailed to the roof for our topping out party. The pitch is a 45 degree angle so snow will have no problem sliding off even tarpaper.

I've traveled to Denver and in one trip purchased a large potbelly stove and a beautiful, working 1912 admiral blue wood cook stove, the latter for only $400. And it's a good thing because I've run out of money. I'm calling my land Huckleberry Hollow, even though they are really Service Berries, pronounced sarvice berries.

It's nearing Thanksgiving and the cabin is about as complete as it will be for this winter. Black tarpaper is on the roof and the plywood is between the six by eights holding the side walls. The floor and walls are fiberglass insulated with plastic on each side and clear plastic covers all the windows, pulled tight by ½ inch wood lath.

There is a loft with a bed on one side by a dormer window and an old hot water tank on the other side I scrounged from the Village Inn at the ski area. I turn on the generator and pump water from the creek to fill the tank on Sundays, providing gravity feed water pressure for the week.

A nearby outhouse has a 55 gallon metal barrel cut in half. I can burn it with diesel when needed, just like in Nam, and not get in trouble for polluting the stream.

My Heart

I have been dating my girlfriend (who doesn't know I call her My Heart in my secret mind) and she has been staying in a house with three others at the ski area. But I have convinced her to move in with me at the rustic cabin in The Hollow.

This may not be a great idea because she is a bit of a free spirit and frequently reminds me how much she enjoys "the preppy look." But I feel certain once she finds out how enchanting it is to live in a forest by a stream she will also fall in love. Sex could not be better, which is not very hard to understand considering the fact that she is proud to relate that she climaxes every time.

Now it is the winter. We park at the end of the road in each of our cars and cross country ski or snowshoe in. The old yellow jeep I've used to haul the wood in with special racks can no longer cut through the snow, even with chains on all four tires in low gear.

We've hit 30 below zero on some nights in January, but I have the potbelly dancing in place. I was smart enough to get 3 tons of hard lump coal and five cords of dry, easy to split ends from the mill for next to nothing. Both stoves take coal and even at zero we sometimes have to leave the Dutch front door open to let cool air in.

I get two channels on a battery powered TV with an antenna in a tree. The generator powers lights and it's fully enclosed to muffle the sound.

The First Winter

The snow is over six feet deep and if you go off the trail we've trampled, you have to dig out of powder snow. On a full moon you can read a book off the snow's reflection. Never in my life have I seen so many stars. And never have I thought love could be so deep. I feel I can reach out and touch the big dipper.

It's late march, below freezing at night, but on this Sunday, Robert his wife and My Heart and I cross country skied four miles upstream, through the empty 600 acres behind the cabin and up into National Forest land. By 1 p.m. it's even too warm for T-shirts in the sun. We stopped for two hours and laid space blankets on the snow in the sun and drank wine with our sandwiches.

As we turned back the sun was lowering quickly. The tracks we made in the snow were starting to ice up and the hour and one half trip up to the hot spot turned into a 15 minute downhill fast glide, flying down to the cabin, occasionally in tuck position. Never has the air smelled so fresh and clean. What joy to be so young with a whole life like this ahead of us. If life gets any better I don't know if I'll be able to handle it.

My garden in the first meadow is step-terraced. By laying a hose in the ditch above it and throwing the end of it out quickly, I can siphon a perfect flow of water to irrigate.

I've given up reporting and am now in charge of advertising and, with a 20% commission, I'm now making twice the money I made as a reporter.

Spring 1977

It's 12 months later and My Heart has a few guys she knew in college up to visit and go cross country skiing from the cabin. But why does she suddenly at the last minute decide to take her top off and go bare-chested like the rest of us. I mean, she's the only girl – my girl. Pangs of jealousy and doubt stab me. Everyone is laughing and having a good time. I am steaming inside. Shouldn't I be proud of the way she looks, tomboy shape notwithstanding? How can she be so proud of herself? So at ease?

Now it's June and My Heart gets a call from her father that he has lined up a job for her with a California congressman serving in Washington, D.C. with a branch office in L.A. She accepts and suddenly I'm standing on my porch while she is packing her car and leaving the Hollow.

I'm frantic. The pain in my chest is like a twisting knife. With no sleep I arrive at the bank the next morning and borrow $700, drive to Denver and fly to Las Vegas. By 11 a.m. I'm parked by the side of the road on I-135 waiting for her car. However long it takes. I know she would have had to spend the night somewhere and would be driving by sometime this afternoon. Hours go by.

A Nevada State Patrol stops behind me and asks what my trouble is. With tears running down my cheeks, I tell him my girlfriend will soon be driving by and I'm going to stop her and ask her to marry me. He tells me, "Good luck."

By 4:30 p.m. I give up. I drive back to Vegas and catch a plane to L.A. My taxi arrives at her father's house about 10 minutes after she has arrived home. I'm in tears, eyes and neck twitching.

"I've just never felt so free in my life," she tells me before I can ask the big question. She and her father tell me to go back to Colorado for the summer so we can both think about how we feel about each other.

Then the owner of the Pilot gives half my advertising accounts to a divorced woman who needed a job and I quit the paper altogether.

Months go by and George and I sit on the bridge watching the brook, day after day. The aspen leaves are rustling and I drink beer, then wine, then Dewar's and water. ½ gram of coke only exaggerates the pain. No man in the world has ever loved a woman as much as I love My Heart. Without her my land means nothing. My life would be a failure.

The leaves are growing dryer and the wind gusts are stronger. The noise is almost deafening, a million leaves yelling at me to go to the coast, to be with her, to tell her how I feel. She will never find another man on this planet with so much love to give. Never!

California Dreaming

It's two weeks before Thanksgiving and my black step side truck is packed. My cabin is rented by a young couple who swear to take good care of George.

I arrive in Santa Monica where she is sharing a narrow white frame house right on the beach with a single guy and girl who are not dating anyone. We're not more than one block north of the Santa Monica pier and every morning I can hear the stupid music from the indoor merry-go-round on the pier.

Almost at once My Heart almost proudly mentions to me that during the summer she has been dating a man who is related to one of America's best known families. But it's B.S. Why would I want to know such a thing? Though, I can't deny, I've certainly heard of him. Well, maybe he's over her. I guess I'm supposed to hope so.

Everyone else goes to work. My Heart works as a press secretary in the L.A. office, although the congressman rarely visits because it's not his main home state office. I read classifieds; mostly help wanted and walk on the beach. I just have to prove myself to be worthy of such love I can't express. I'm somebody at my cabin; here I feel worthless.

My Heart introduces me to an older man, I'll call Sil, who teaches aerial skiing and is an expert roller skater. He scores me a pair of 4-wheel skates and I begin skating every day. Soon I'm skating several miles down to Venice Beach with all the freaks and back again, once, twice, three times a day. Weight lifters, chain saw jugglers, bikini and thong skaters and pickpockets and shuckers and jivers.

Weeks later I've muscled out a possible screen play for Sil about snow skiers who do aerials called "Double Twisting Back flip". We even have a connection with a producer at one of the major film studios, but it's quickly dismissed as being "too reportage".

I then have a brilliant idea of a book or possibly a screenplay about a boy who is part American Indian who grows up high in the mountains of Colorado who has a remarkable gift: he has the fastest reactions of anyone in the world. I mean if a teacher were to drop a pencil, he would be able to dart from his desk and catch it before it hit the ground. He certainly couldn't be tackled in football because he would be able to dodge and evade any grab. And good luck trying to hit him in a fight.

I figure all the skinny guys in the world could relate to it because one doesn't have to lift weights or be built strong to really succeed in life. And it seemed like a good dream. I've decided to call my book, "Tommy Feathersmith...the boy with the fastest reactions."

I was so excited I even sent copies of rough outlines to myself, garnishing a "poor man's copyright" buy not opening the dated envelopes. Needless to say I wasn't going to be making any money off this idea in the near future and My Heart was not enthused at all. I rather quickly decided to table the whole idea.

A small bar next to the Santa Monica Pier has an in-crowd of Hollywood old-timer extras, a few of which I vaguely seem to remember. They play cards and chess. The owner/bartender keeps riff raff away by not recognizing their existence if they come over to order.

I met a bespectacled guy at a bar in Venice Beach and had an intense 10 minute conversation with him. I convinced him to walk back to see where I live, and he kept talking the whole way about how "you've got to have a dream and really, really believe in it. Then you can't let anything stop you."

He looked at the outside of the white house where we lived and then said, "You've got to believe in your dream."

As he was walking away I said, "What's your name?"

"Steven Spielberg," he said. Never heard of him, I thought, but I'm sure he'll make it big, if he's not too much of a dreamer.

In February I interviewed for a job out of the newspaper and showed up at a one-story office in Santa Monica where the owner looked at my resume and liked the Vietnam veteran part. I met him the next day and we drove around to a number of new and used car dealerships where he dropped off paperwork for "Extended Service Contracts." Apparently he was freelancer who split the $350 to $500 charge customers paid to dealers for the contracts. I asked him if it was insurance company backed and he said, "No, that's the beauty of it. There's almost never really a payout. Maybe a couple of times."

Apparently in small print, it was a "breakdown Policy" extended service contract. The vehicle owner has to actually break down on the highway to be covered. If someone hears a strange noise and drives back to the dealer to have it checked out, the contract isn't valid. He didn't actually break down.

"Anyway, the new cars have a manufacturers warrantee to cover drive trains and anything major so what's the difference."

I didn't show up for work the next day, but wrote a newspaper article about how illegal the whole thing seemed to be. Then I took it down to the L.A. Herald Examiner newspaper and talked my way up to the news desk. After showing it to an editor, the news desk copy editor asked me what I wanted for the article. I said nothing, just a shot at a job. I was hired on for a two-week trial starting the next day. They never ran the article.

My second day on the job I was sent down to the courthouse to see what was going on with a divorce case being held in closed chambers between Jack Kent Cooke and his wife. A little research showed Cooke had holdings including the Los Angeles Lakers, Los Angeles Kings, the Forum and four-fifths of the Washington Redskins, worth about 75 million, plus two million shares of Teleprompter.

A court clerk was quick to lead me to three push carts of boxes of files pertaining to the divorce. There were plenty of accusations from both sides, including drinking, shoving and shouting. Plus one file stated that on a Sunday when Cooke was supposed to have broken his arm playing touch football, his wife actually had tried to run him over with her Cadillac.

I chatted with Cooke's chauffer for an hour who wouldn't say a thing except what a great guy his boss was. Then as the lawyers and Cooke and his wife came out of the judge's chambers, I approached them with some of the information I had read. The lawyers pulled me aside and told me if I didn't print anything in the newspaper about what I read in the divorce filings, they would give me an exclusive interview when a settlement was reached.

The Examiner quickly agreed to the terms and I spent the next several days just sitting around the courthouse. Finally I was told an agreement was reached and the paper sent a more experienced reporter down to help me with the interview. The lawyers first tried to give us no information but my seasoned assistant broke into a blue streak swearing frenzy about the broken promise and how she would rake the lawyers over the coals and would make sure everyone knew what their cut of the action was going to be.

They opened up and we had a front page story about what was believed to be the largest divorce settlement in U.S. history:

"Sports Baron Jack Kent Cooke, 66, who once sold encyclopedias door-to-door but later, amassed a fortune estimated at $100 million, yesterday agreed to split his property with his ex-wife in what may be the largest divorce settlement ever."

He later had to sell the L.A. Lakers to satisfy the settlement, but kept the Washington Redskins.

As it turned out, however, the paper said I only had experience on a weekly paper and wasn't fast enough at rewrite, so I only lasted another week at the paper.

It's Over

Now I am more depressed than ever. I spend my days roller
skating back and forth to Venice Beach. I even wear an old tuxedo
my father gave me complete with a black derby hat when I skate
on the beach. I even get a little applause in addition to the stares.
I'm just as good skating backwards as forward and I've got spins
down pretty good. If I see a bench or someone lying down on
the sidewalk, I just jump over them. I could probably put my hat
down and people would throw coins into it. I just don't care about
anything.

My Heart sometimes comes home way late at night. And she
even has to fly to places like Washington D.C. Then one evening
I get a call while she is spending a weekend in San Francisco and
she tells me over the phone that it would be best if I went back to
Steamboat.

Of course like a fool, I go over to her mother's house and cry
my heart out about how much I love her. Two of her sisters come in
the room to watch my pathetic scene.

Then there's nothing left to do but pack up my black pickup,
score a half gram of coke on credit I'll never pay back and begin my
tearful journey back to Colorado. I realize I'm basically worthless
and I've lost the only thing I ever really loved in my life. Even the
prospect of going home to my land and my dog doesn't brighten the
gloom of my nothingness.

Ode To Love

When I think in evening's breeze
and when the night is cool and still,
flowers, my darling, bursting petals
explode in my head and all thoughts
of life swirl so thick I nearly faint
as in kaleidoscope magic you appear.

Oh, your breath upon my face,
your golden arms around my waist
whisper soft my love, there is
no time, oh, god no end.
Only now, now, now
repeating in throbbing joy.

My whole life means nothing,
a shadow of a form,
that of energy, in swirling planes,
in twirling bliss
I cease to be
when thee I kiss.

Old English, ancient frock
robe of Athens, African shower.
A thousand shades of green with
uncountable drops of life.
Steaming heat rises to the skies.
Love of life is my gift to thee.

When I dream upon the silent waters
lapping at the shore
Flowers, darling, bursting petals
explode in my head
so thick I nearly faint
from the joy of it all

When I dream upon the rushing torrents
of waters in the rivers
or babbling brooks and streams
I catch my breath in wonder
at the beauty of it all.

And when I picture foaming waters
swirling in the sea
my thoughts all turn to pleasure,
and a life of you and me.

Home Again

I've been living at a friend's house for six weeks because I can't get the couple to move out of my cabin until June. Basically I am a shadow of my previous form and spend too much time in the bars. Working back at the paper seems out of the question. I can't go back.

I'm back to becoming a carpenter and jobsite grunt, just like I did in high school. At least George and I have the cabin. My schedule consists of working and drinking during the week, then stocking up for a weekend alone where I hide out. I am finally reading all of the books I have been accumulating over the years.

But how many times can I reread "Autobiography of a Guru" by Paramhansa Yogananda? Enough to know there is something going on in this universe. I promptly pack up all my existential theory of life crap. Even if I do use books as extra insulation on my walls.

To a Lonely Existentialist

> Untold dreams of childhood revisited
>   reflect upon my soul,
> and haunt my tarnished membrane shell
>   in latent evening's toll.
> Inspirations we put off,
>   unchecked and left to whither,
> will all be recollected, I fear,
>   before life's one last quiver.
> But still we say the mirror is mute,
>   no regret in personal treason.
> And so we sit, and wait to die
>   as in Sartre's "Age of Reason."

****

It is the Fall

The months are sliding by. It is late fall again. Always the fall. I pound on the typewriter and if I don't drink too much or get too high some of it seems to make sense. But where the thoughts are coming from I know not. Just shreds of self-pity.

Some days I simply lie on the couch and meditate. Now I have a fear of heights, no sense of humor and no self-confidence. One day I am so depressed I feel I should just end it all. Life doesn't seem to be worth living. I am floating ten feet over myself, looking down as I've always done since my early days of childhood when I used to float over to the knot holes in the pine paneled room.

But suddenly I hear a faint voice calling me, first from far away, then growing stronger. It's the voice of my mother calling… "James…James…time to come home for dinner."

I was floating higher now and was actually above the roof. Then I was suddenly only ten feet above the ground and I was floating over the brook, only upright as though I was walking, but not moving my legs.

I could smell the grass and wildflowers with stunning fragrance. And, besides the babbling water over stones in the brook I could hear a rich humming sound as though the earth itself was emitting a delightful rumble as it turned on its axis.

I had no fear of height and my only sense of air was heat from the sun. Then, in a whisper, I was back within myself on the couch.

Was this real or imagined? Did this change me? No, I still felt depressed and worthless. And yet, I suddenly felt as though I had to go on living. Either the Earth or Nature or some sort of spirit loved me enough to show me there is something going on beyond what most people think. I was given some sense of hope. Perhaps all my ancestors were emitting energy, giving me a sense of power.

Of course I knew if I ever started telling people about what I experienced, they were sure to tell me I've gone crazy and it was time to lock me up. But, what are these thoughts that keep entangling my mind?

****

Hippies don't love life: they love their minds.
Hippies have fallen in love with their minds.

****

Non-love met non-hate and discussed the nothingness of it all.

****

Socialist countries tax whisky so heavy one has to be rich to be able to afford to be drunk. But how long can even a rich drunk survive?

****

Met this guy who said that while stoned on acid, he saw the whole universe when he opened a rancid jar of mayonnaise on a shelf in a cupboard. He said his whole life flashed before him and he bent over like a bull and roared out of the room. But, we all said, that was his karma.

****

Although I once reflected esoteric innocence incensed the incense inside an insolent infinitesimal, insisting I instead implore essence in isolated ideas, irrationally unconceived, ironically evading all incinerary ideologists endeavors, I never really would have guessed it: you can't write while stoned.

****

A god forgives and forgets.
Man forgets but doesn't forgive.

****

How can the absurd be so beautiful? I lived in a tree fort in the happiest moments of my life.

****

A few months later I heard My Heart was in town. She even came to visit me, but only stayed for an hour. She still really likes me, but is dating around a bit, trying to make up her mind. And she is enjoying her freedom.

A Snowy Trip

It has been a few weeks since my floating experience and I was still trying to comprehend what it all means when I received a frantic call from my neighbor Robert. He had sold a painting his uncle left him and had just scored a full ounce of "the best quality coke ever. Totally uncut."

Robert had one small problem, however – the DEA was on to him, watching his house, and he needed help immediately.

I hurried over and found a guy I'll call Bogie, because his mannerism, speech and build are nearly identical to Humphrey Bogart, and two other casual acquaintances I knew, and they were all armed. There was no way the narcs could get a warrant to come into his house, Robert stated in a hushed whisper, but they most certainly would try to look through the windows and thereby have enough cause to enter and bust him.

Our job, I was informed, was to guard the perimeters of the property throughout the rest of the day and through the night and in return we would have free coke in whatever amount was needed. We all agreed it was a very reasonable offer. Then, at first light, Robert was going to make a run for it and hide the remaining stash under a fence post somewhere in a glass jar.

Robert then proceeded to clear off his rather infamous four-foot diameter glass top circular coffee table. I wasn't sure if I could remember the number of times someone had attempted to flip a small vial with gold spoon attached across this table, only to find a missed catch resulted in the shattering of the glass container. On those occasions coke had to be strained through a silk stocking which may or may not have removed all shards of glass.

Using a ruler, Robert proceeded to chop and cut out six 10-inch long lines including one for his faithful wife, and I was already contact high in anticipation before a neatly rolled $100 bill secured by a rubber band made its way to my kneeling form. Given that I promptly snorted five inches on each side and given the quality of the product I could barely maintain my senses by the time the first

It is the Fall

beers were cracked and the first cigarettes were fired up.

We were all so totally stoned that no one felt like going outside until after sunset, never mind the fact that no one had even questioned just what exactly we were supposed to do if we encountered a federal agent or two. Apparently we were just to stand up with a loaded gun pointing at them and say, "Excuse me, but this is private property, nothing is going on so you'll just have to move along." I couldn't even imagine what any of our eyes would look like under the scrutiny of a flashlight.

So at dusk, three of us, bent over like trotting hunchbacks, went to our pre-determined positions: two in the trees about 80 years from the house and one in the ditch along county road 36. We each had a pistol and two of us had shotguns. Needless to say, all was still quiet around 9 p.m., with the exception of a few cars with bright headlights speeding along the road. There was no moon or it was so clouded over we couldn't see it, which would be quite unusual at this elevation.

At 9:30 p.m. we all dashed back to the cabin as agreed upon. It felt like we had pulled an all-nighter and our throats were so dry we could hardly swallow. We had been on patrol for all of one hour. We crowded the table snorting the cut out lines and our eyes looked like paratroopers being ordered to jump out of a plane. Robert and Bogie pulled the next shift, with Robert's wife rapidly repeating, "Be careful...don't take any chances!"

After two more shift changes we all were convinced that there were at least six to eight narcs across the road, behind several trees and slowly closing in behind moving bushes. If there had been just one tumbleweed I was convinced there would have been a massive firefight with all of us shooting at each other.

Still, all things considered, given our stoned states of mind, I was fairly convinced we would make it until dawn until the almost predictable shock wave hit. Robert decided to roll the snorting bill just a little tighter so we wouldn't be snorting such honkers, and when he removed the rubber band, sure enough, a crisp $10 bill had magically replaced the hundred. The accusations and denials were enough to break solid bonds of friendship, had we all not finally agreed that there must have been some kind of mistake. It was several days later before Robert found a rolled $100 between the couch cushions and realized perhaps he had made a switch before one of his night patrols.

I drifted home shortly after dawn and slept for 14 hours. I didn't have the nerve to ask if there was really very much of the stash left to take to the fence post burial.

Spring

I made it through the winter and finally the snow is melting and I can hear boulders – large rocks actually – rumbling down the creek. I sit on the deck and the ever-present ache in my stomach is there again.

A few more months pass and then...one day the phone rings. It is My Heart.

"James," she says, seeming so far away. "I've been fired." Then, a long pause.

"What are you going to do?" I ask, almost nonchalantly.

"I'm thinking of coming back there..."

"I don't know" I said, looking out the beveled glass windows at the brook. "I don't know if that would be a good idea. I'm not sure if you're the girl I could spend the rest of my life with; I mean I don't think you would ever love me enough."

There is a long pause. Finally. "Oh, James," My Heart says. Pause.

"Yea. I guess I'll see you around," I say, the words stinging in my mouth.

There is a long pause. Then we both hang up.

Should I call her back? No. She hurt me too much. If she really loves me she will come out to my land and tell me. Maybe it's just my land she loves anyway. Certainly not me. Not after all I've been through. She'll have to come out and beg me to take her back, even though I'm the one in so much pain. I'll just wait for her. How can she not love the life we had and what lies before us?

Why didn't I chase after her? And who were all those other men she's been with? Why didn't she love me then? It's no use. I have no money and no real job. Suddenly I feel bitterness instead of love. What's wrong with me? Am I going crazy? Or is it just that I feel as though I could never satisfy her. Not after those good looking guys.

Days pass. Then a week. I keep looking up the road to see

if I can see her walking up the road toward the Hollow. Arms outstretched. And I see that great big smile on her face.

It's been a month and sometimes George and I hear a sound. We walk quickly to the front door, gaze out toward the road, looking for My Heart. Sometimes at night under the moon we look out, but this time it is just a hoot owl. He's lived here now for three years.

I tell no one she's called. And who would believe me anyway? Not even Robert. I just keep repeating to myself what was said over the phone.

It's no longer what it was; it's what it could have been. I'm living a dream. And it's not even a good dream. I only know I'll never give my heart to anyone again. I couldn't handle the pain again. I'm just too weak. Too insecure.

****

A rock lays still on barren soil
 where once I knew a wall.
That log with ants and burrowed holes
 once held a mighty roof.
And over there, that dying oak
 once squeaked with rope and swing.
Tell me of your hopes, old man,
 back when your father was alive.

The 1980s

I've landed a job at the Hayden Power Plant, a coal-burning electrical generating station located 20 miles from Steamboat. I've started out as a utility man which means I go wherever physical labor is needed.

I've actually had some shifts where for eight hours straight my whole job consists of pushing a broom, sweeping fine coal dust into little piles. The hardest part of the job is the shift work: 5 days, followed by 7 swings and 5 graveyard shifts.

I'm promoted to operator and I spend my shift going to every moving piece of equipment and checking gauges and pressure valves, looking for leaks or warning sounds. We stay in touch with other operators and the control room by walkie-talkies. Sometimes we drive in pickups around the plant and it's not unusual to catch short catnaps on graveyard shifts.

The swing shifts are best because by getting off at midnight it's still possible to make it back to town for a couple of last call drinks, or even catch a last set if a band plays late.

I've even met a girl, a divorced woman actually, with two children, at a new bar in town called the Longbranch. We seem to hit it off at once and I find myself staying at her house when I'm unwilling or unable to make it back to the cabin. She is to become My Angel because of the many times she has saved me from making a fool of myself.

On days off from the power plant George wags his tail and looks at me with those brown eyes, knowing we're going to spend a few days together at the cabin with rum and cokes a bottle of wine and, after pay day, with a half a gram. I use the old Ed Sullivan dog act trick of giving him little squares of yellow cheese when he answers my questions with the right amount of enthusiasm.

There was a small fire in one of the coal grinders on the shift before I got to work. A young operator received permission from someone in the control room to stick a water hose into the grinder to put out the fire. An explosion instantly blew the side out and shrapnel hit his chest killing him. A few guys picketed for a couple of days but no one was really going to walk off the job and lose their fat pay check.

I've quit my job at the power plant after 18 months but figured out a way to get unemployment so I can actually cruise around town like other young fat cats. I also go over to Bogies house when he gets an ounce of coke, often by Fed Ex from Aspen where he once lived. I help him cut up little squares from slick magazines so bindles can be passed on to friends.

There are a number of other small cliques of friends around town doing the same thing. It's not like anyone is actually dealing, in the sense of making money. Just friends getting some good stash at cost so the one taking the risk can get a little for free. Of course, the quality of some coke is so good that it would be a disservice to everyone if it was put on the street in such a high quality state. Thus steps had to be taken to make the cocaine more acceptable.

Anycitol tablets are sometimes ground up to powder and baked in the oven to shine nicely. Some resort to mannitol or manite, or forms of baby laxative. Baking soda is more preferred to rub on the gums for a good numbing high. No one seems surprised to see members of both sexes going to bathrooms together even though they may have only recently met.

When on a runner, I've found myself darting into the ladies room at bars or restaurants like the Brandywine, reaching above the mirror and finding a bindle which I politely only take one or two small little fingernail bites into. I suppose an employee would have a sense of job security if he were to be the one supplying small bindles to a boss or owner.

If I'm dining at the Butcher shop restaurant at the ski area, I've found that if I ask a certain waiter for a special dessert, I will find a half gram under my ice cream dish on the saucer. Naturally a fifty will discreetly take its place when I ask the waiter to remove my dessert.

Back at the cabin, I spend my spare time pecking at the typewriter or writing thoughts and phrases in rambling longhand. Sometimes loneliness is a good thing. Time, even life itself, goes by so much slower. It's as though I've been given more free time and months to live than others who keep busy in conversation. It's a way of staying young, not aging if your head is in the right place. Maybe I will be able to emerge from this cocoon substantially younger than others at my age.

The Middle 80s

I've finally gone completely straight. I realized a couple of years ago that I never really enjoyed the pot high. It was always just peer pressure making me indulge when a joint is passed around. I haven't even done coke in over a year. Although I've never drank alcohol before or during a job, I am still what's called a "functioning alcoholic." I mean I still have five quick drinks after work to get the escape high, even though I don't know what I'm "escaping," except, of course, all my insecurities and weaknesses.

Then again, I am still dealing with the fact that if I am perfectly straight and laying on the couch and meditating, I am still able to float slowly over my property. It always starts with being just ten feet or so over my prone body, then slowly rising up and through the roof, then back closer to the ground. I'm quite afraid of leaving my property in this state or being seen, as if this were even possible. It's very weird because I know I am not dreaming but I certainly do not dare to tell anyone and I don't feel enlightened really. I still have my nervous neck and eye twitches so I don't know how this experience is helping me in any way. I don't even dare mentioning any of this to my girlfriend, My Angel.

In the meantime, I have spent the past several years working as a waiter at several restaurants including a new, small pizza place in a little mall off Highway 40. I handle the in-house five tables, but fast delivery is the specialty, besides the super thin cracker-like crust and great sauce. Word spread quickly at motel and rental condo front desks that every 10 pizza referrals is good for a free pizza to the desk. During the first winter we kept three drivers hopping from 4 p.m. to midnight.

The next summer the owner sold the place to a newly arrived couple from the Midwest with two children who sold two Kentucky Fried Chicken franchises to move to Steamboat. Besides overpaying, they hired high school kids for deliveries and to work in the kitchen and apparently didn't know about the free pizza entitlements. I think they went under the next year.

My friend Robert recently returned from a full 30-day rehab at a well-known clinic near Minneapolis which he hinted cost a cool ten grand. I can only wish him the best as he hopes to continue building log homes primarily with timbers of beetle-killed pine from the Yampa mill.

I've got a part-time job at the Bud Werner Memorial Library. What can be better than being around books all day? It's the best job ever! It's worth being straight and dealing with an educated public. The best part is when someone asks a question or needs a specific answer. It's as though I'm the reference librarian at the Smithsonian. Of course for now it's just a small A-frame building next to the sulfur springs with very old books.

Memories

Sometimes when I am alone in my cabin I try to think back at some of the good times I had in the '60s and '70s. I remember there was no cover at the Cantina to see a band from Texas called ZZ Top. Then there was the frantic drive to Boulder in 1966 to score a couple of lids at the Sink or Tulagi bars. It was 4 p.m. and I heard a band across the street practicing a song that started with the line, "Well, I woke up this morning, and you were on my mind…" I remember seeing the We Five later on television.

Then there was the time there was a giant fish tank between the bar and the dining area at the Pub downtown. The owners thought it would be cool to put a few piranha fish in the tank. Then, during the lunch rush, they tossed in a few large goldfish at what they called feeding time. Somehow, the older customers didn't enjoy dining while they watched the goldfish swimming around with just their heads and their body skeletons remaining. It didn't help that the few customers at the bar were screaming in delight and yelling in high-pitched voices, "Help…help. Save me someone."

I remember meeting Phoebe Snow who did quite well with one of the greatest voices ever, and Mary McGregor spending a winter singing "Torn Between Two Lovers" at the Inn at Thunderhead at the base of the ski area. And I remember writing the obit for local musician Anthony who died falling out of a hang glider over Mt. Werner in 1975.

It was in the '70s that I first put a sign on my cabin door reading, "Warning: Radar beam intrusion detector and battery powered anti-personnel device in use. Trespass at your own risk." And I thought I was so cool with a checkbook that listed me as The Baron of Huckleberry Hollow, Strawberry Park, Steamboat Springs.

My Best Friend

It's another spring day in early April and my dog George can no longer make it up the steps to the cabin, or even walk in two feet of snow in the shade. After 15 years I realize it's time to put him down. For the last few years I have been giving him a prednisone pill daily with cheese and this seemed to relieve any pain from hip problems. But the vet told me it's not in his best interest for me to be carrying him up steps and I must face the decision.

I can't make the drive myself to the veterinarian, so My Angel has graciously agreed to do it for me. I can only sit at my desk in the cabin and stare at his empty backpack.

****

Not a Purebred

You old unsightly pug-faced cur,
callus-soled independent runner
of the night-eyes race:
you never fetched a stick
and brought it back,
rarely came when called
lest hunger beckoned.
You mud-pawed suits and shirts and rugs,
you tail-shattered mother's vase.
Licking stranger's hands
and panting foul breath on all who came to chat.
I kicked you good when you bit the neighbor girl's hand
(though she grabbed your tail).

And through it all,
those 15 years of cold and lean
in mountain cabin's warmth,

your wet brown eyes gazed my way
ten thousand times and more,
begging faith and taking hope,
those hours seem now too fast.
Yes, dear brown dog,
you good-for-nothing mongrel mutt,
I guess I loved you more than my hand could show.
For through it all, rejection or a pet,
I know now my strange affection
that kept me to your cause:
you were my friend.

****

The library board hired an official director last year with a degree in library science from the Midwest who is generous with praise and extremely easy to work with. Being short, attractive and with pleasant, expressive eyes I felt sure she would upgrade the meager volume of new books available.

Not only do we now have books just listed on the New York Times best seller list, a whole new wing, larger than the original library itself is being built. It's hard to look at her without thinking of a young Irene Dunne.

The Waiting Game

A new, small restaurant with a five stool bar called Scotty's BBQ has opened adjacent to the courthouse jail and I've landed a job to supplement my income. There are only between 8 and 10 tables depending on configuration, but the BBQ is totally authentic.

Carl, the owner, has brought recipes he acquired from a smokehouse restaurant near Tioga, Texas. 15 pound slabs of beef brisket are smoked for 2 ½ days over oak and mesquite he has trucked up by a friend from Texas. Baby back ribs are smoked about 14 hours and the customer puts on his own amount of our special barbeque sauce served in Groulch beer bottles with rubber stoppers. We push Groulch at the restaurant but the customer has to leave the bottle behind.

There's also smoked beans, black-eyed peas and deep-fried okra and fries, not to mention smoked sausage and cole slaw. Carl and his buddy Doug and I get a system down quickly. Ribs and brisket are reheated in microwave ovens and we can turn tables fast. The first winter it's not unusual to have lines waiting in the hallway and outside and tips are flowing fast.

I am totally straight at the library, but at 5:30 p.m. when I arrive at the BBQ house job, I quickly down three stiff rum and cokes to change into the comedic waiter. I am treading water again. I don't love myself enough to achieve the joy I want to experience in this life.

There is something wrong with the bond between my land and my dreams being unfulfilled. After more than nine years, I realize I have never made love with My Angel on my property. She has never even spent a night with me at my cabin. Even worse, it is 1989 and this fall I will be 45 years old. My life is more than half over and I am too old to desire having children.

I also just realized that I haven't been to the base of the ski area in more than 3 years. New, fresh young people keep arriving in town and I really have nothing in common with them. And they all seem to have unlimited funds, even just out of college, or even high school.

I am reminded of a poem by W.B. Yeats from The Tower, 1938, called Sailing to Byzantium, thinking of it as Sailing to Steamboat Springs: "That is no country for old men. The young, in one another's arms, birds in the trees, those dying generations at their song…an aged man is but a paltry thing, a tattered coat upon a stick, unless soul clap its hands and sing…"

Another Trip

Today, for the first time, I concentrated on floating to a spot not above my property. After some time, I was instantly in the middle of Strawberry Park, at the junction of county road 36 and the road to Buffalo Pass.

I was perhaps 200 feet overhead, though again with no fear of height. I have no idea what time it was, but it was shortly after I had heard the noon whistle even from the safety of my couch. And then, as I looked down, I saw a person walking toward the old Swinehart house.

I can't explain how this could be possible, but: I actually saw my shadow on the ground ahead of the strolling individual! "This can't be!" I thought. And I saw him turn to look up towards me. But I was directly in front of the sun…he shielded his eyes, but was obviously blinded by the bright glare.

In an instant I was home. Back on my couch. But my heart was pounding incessantly, louder and faster than I've ever known. I thought I was going to have a heart attack. I only knew one thing: I must sell my land and move on.

And I must tell no one. Not that anyone would believe me, I knew. But I made a pact with myself.

Moving On

I have decided to sell my property and move on to save myself...or better yet to find myself. I need to start fresh again and not dwell on what might have been.

My neighbor Robert has been to a rehab center again, although he admitted he snuck in a supply of hash in his belt buckle to get him through the "rough spots" of relating problems to others in his group. I fear he still needs the alcohol as a daily medication. But who am I to judge?

In the days following the listing of my land, I am feeling joy and relief. Last night, under a full moon, I floated with the white owl for what seemed like hours among the hundreds of tall pine trees behind my cabin. We darted between the tree trunks and up through the boughs. I know if I were to relate this to anyone they would certainly brush it off as only a dream. I also know a white owl is not considered to be a very good omen.

I have found I can only float to a spot I have been before, for I now believe wherever we travel, each of us leaves small parts of matterless energy behind. Thus, our minds can always recall in perfect detail places we have visited, just by instantly calling upon energy to return to our brain.

I can recall energy from my visit through Europe, to the Vatican Museum, or the Louvre in Paris, or even looking up at the ceiling in the Sistine Chapel. I can revisit any museum I have been to, from room to room either from my couch, or by going there with my mind. But I cannot explain that shadow on the ground, nor do I even want to think about it anymore. I just want to be free, like traveling through the pines.

I only know there is something going on here on Earth and it seems far greater than some theory of evolution. It's as though every thought of every creature one's mind could imagine has already appeared here on earth, or at least any that would have a chance of survival.

To Tell A Tree

I can tell a tree by its leaf
   or by its bark,
and some, I would suppose, could even
   by the root determine
the make and model of countless species
   of the tall and shady
wood-and-heat-providing leafy growth
   that, as a rule, has the
fortitude to outlive man.

And yet how difficult to tell
   a tree the real truth
of how I love it, really care,
   and would, if I could,
take time to share, exchange the thoughts
   and knowledge of origins
and history, of dreams and goals
   past and present,
and of mutual lovings of dawns and dusks,
   and countless daybreaks
warmed and nurtured by loving sun
   beaming her rays on Mother Earth.

The only way, I would suppose, to tell
   a tree of love and need
is by cultivation, nourishment of soil
   (food for sap, in truth, its blood)
and by careful pruning, selective cutting,
   breaking away of dead branches and,
for future preservation of the genus species,
   leaving air and water pure as can be.

How odd, then, to suddenly contemplate
    that when we pollute,
we kill a tree, and many other plants and shrubbery
    less majestic in their stance:
we are, in truth, causing pain and disrespect
    not only to ourselves but to so many other
living things less vocal and demanding,
    lacking in political clout
but possessing, perhaps, all the rights and beauty
    and planet life-supporting need that
our very life itself could not survive without.

****

The realtor has found a buyer for my land, a nice couple, obviously well off, who I believe will be good custodians. They will build a big house, like I once dreamed, on the garden spot and will surely remove all traces of my rustic cabin. I have seen it in my mind, and the only trace of where I lived will be a large patch of wildflowers.

For now, I can only dream of winters on a small island in the Caribbean, snorkeling and scuba diving in 80 degree water. I know it won't be on any of the U.S. Virgin Islands. And I long for fly fishing the Salmon and Snake Rivers and floating the River of No Return in Idaho and maybe floating the Middle Fork of the Salmon at its peak in June.

I also know the truth of the supposed Indian legend that every long-time local is convinced he made up: "Once you see the seasons change in Steamboat you leave part of your soul there and you will always come back to find it."

The memories of my property must remain just that physically. I know I can easily revisit any part of the Hollow any time I wish in my own way. That fact, and my memories are all a man, a young boy really, could ever expect. I wish everyone the best, and good health, and a long life.

As for me, it is my desire to never grow up.

I must be off my land by Christmas, but for now, I still must face this incessant desire to figure out my mind and how to best use it.

While Loving Leaves

A hammock, stretched between two trees, stretched out over a brook. It's nearing evening. It is the fall. I'm lying in the hammock.

Hair down to my waist – no, to my feet – it is overflowing out of the hammock, into the stream and over the sides of the bank. And the past again flashing back. What is truth and what is imagination? Who said there's any difference? I forgot his name.

Leaves are floating down. Several land on me and I study one of them for a long while, turning it slowly through my fingers. Then I put it in my mouth and eat it: crunch-a-munch-a-dust.

I fought in many wars
and had many loves and lives,
I even touched the moon
while lying in my hammock
on a lazy afternoon.

TOMMY FEATHERSMITH...

...the boy with the fastest reactions in the world

By James

WHEN DAWN BREAKS over the Colorado Rockies, slivers of sunlight thread themselves through pine needles in streams of white light. And as the sun breaks over the horizon, the slivers of light take on prism hues in the billions of drops of dew clinging to every pine needle and blade of grass.

IT IS STILL COLD, even in the summer months, at dawn at 9,000 feet, but the body of Tommy Feathersmith is glistening in sweat. Clad in only a leather loincloth and headband, he runs along a stream, then up a steep hill into a stand of lodge pole pine. Dead branches fly in all directions as he knocks them off with feet and hands, spinning and kicking as though against so many adversaries. The sound of a solitary tom-tom and an old man chanting an Indian song grows louder and Tommy seems to be running to the beat.

ACROSS AN OPEN FIELD, the youth smiles and laughs as he runs. A rabbit is scared up and Tommy darts and chases it for 50 yards until he dives into the open grass.

AT A CABIN near a small brook the White One sits on the porch playing a tom-tom and chanting an Indian song. Now in his 70s, his white hair flows over his shoulders, and his eyes gaze higher in the sky as direct sunlight breaks over a peak and shines on his face. He is one-fourth Indian but looks it only in his nose and face. He knows it will soon be his time to enter the next world.

ABRUPTLY he stops playing and stares downstream. His eyes squint as he hears a pebble brush a rock in the brook. A hand moves slowly from behind the corner of the cabin and reaches for the old man's neck. Instantly he grabs the wrist, which grabs his and the two left wrists then block and parry in blinding speed, then freeze, holding each other's forearms.

"Were the rabbits fast today?" White One, the boy's father asks, even before viewing the catch. "I only saw one," Tommy says, getting the rabbit, which is cleaned and stretched on sticks.

They talk quietly before the rising sun; behind them pelts glisten. The youth will be 16 in the fall – only a month away – and the old man tells him he must leave then to begin his journey into the world. He has learned much from the 300 books the White One brought with him to the cabin.

The boy also knows the secrets of the circle of life in nature, and his tests and trials alone in the woods have taught the youth to overcome fear. He has also learned of the "time zones" of life which make some days, hours or seconds pass at different speeds for different men...and animals, as well. People in one area at a given time may be all moving at a faster or slower speed than others elsewhere. But clocks will read the same at both areas.

They go inside the cabin which contains a large cook stove from which the old man pulls out freshly baked bread as the boy makes tea with dried herbs. The walls are lined with books which Tommy has memorized; they have been his primary source of education since his mother passed on. Using his lightning speed, he can read pages almost at a scan. In another state he can pass exams to go right to senior year in high school...and beyond if he wishes. Far away, he won't be known as the son of a crazy man.

The boy and his father live on one of the few remaining privately owned 640 acre sections within this area of the national forest. Less than eight miles north of Hahn's Peak near Clark, Colorado, they possess a well-kept secret: a small but steady trickle of water in a cave on their property produces tiny flakes of gold from an underground source that may well be the undiscovered mother lode never located within the towering Hahn's Peak. Only once a year has the old man traveled to an assessor's office in Nevada to cash in leather pouches of gold dust.

It is these funds which will provide income for Tommy's unique journey through life. For him to take a physical job or even play sports such as football would call too much attention to his lightning fast speed. He would be impossible to tackle in football. And when his mother had him attending school, even in the second grade, sitting in the front row, when his teacher dropped a pencil, he leaped from his desk and caught it before it could strike the floor. Home schooling was the only choice for his own protection...and that of others.

Later, Tommy began removing square pieces of sod and brush in front of a steep hillside. Looking inside he viewed the old black pickup truck with stock racks and brand new tires.

Driving down a winding gravel road, the truck turns onto a two-lane highway, but is stopped shortly by a county sheriff's car.

"Haven't seen you since spring, Tommy," the deputy says. "You get that driver's license yet?" Though friends, the deputy seems determined to enforce the law this time.

Suddenly, trucks come barreling down the road from both directions. Looking both ways, Tommy throws the deputy onto the hood of his truck and jumps out of the way just as the semi-trailers pass each other adjacent to the pickup, horns blaring, with only inches to spare. The officer would have been run over. He tells Tommy he can have two days grace in town.

To be (most likely) never continued...